Broken
By
Evil

By

Dr. Jeri Fink

and

Donna Paltrowitz

Photography by Dr. Jeri Fink
Cover and book design by Derek Murphy

Broken By Evil
Written By Dr. Jeri Fink & Donna Paltrowitz
Photographs By Dr. Jeri Fink
Book and cover design By Derek Murphy

Published By Book Web Publishing, LTD
Copyright © 2014 By Book Web Publishing, LTD
All Rights reserved

ISBN: 978-1-941882-08-5

For Ricky
and all the people in my life who bring me joy, insight,
and a world of imagination

1941-2008

Broken

By

Evil

Espie

1

What next?

Efraym, deep in thought, was reluctant to go home. He was terrified and excited, looking forward to the future and at the same time, dreading it. The Bronx streets blurred as he wandered – voices and madness were muted. His greatest prayer had been answered at the same time that The Great Depression sucked out his soul.

Millions of people grappled with the same question. Everyone knew that their lives and the world would never be the same. Few knew what was next.

"It's crazy to start a family *now*," his friend, Isaac, frowned. "What were you thinking?"

Efraym and his wife had been trying to have a baby for ten years. Ironically, the child was conceived when the country was in its greatest crisis. No one was thinking about a new family in 1941; they were focused on survival.

Efraym forgot to watch where he was going. He turned onto the wrong street. There were streets for Irish, Jews, Ukrainians, and Italians. You stayed on your street or asked for trouble. Efraym was too distracted to realize he was on Irish turf.

An Irish kid sitting on a stoop glared at the Jew.

People had lost everything. New Yorkers gasped for air as if they still lived in the old country. Eyes were hollow, faces gaunt, and clothes patched. Hoovervilles rose in Central Park, along the Hudson River and in the auto dump yards. The shantytowns were built by homeless families using garbage. The men turned away in shame; the women clutched pitifully thin, wailing children. The only way Efraym could help was to avoid their eyes – not acknowledge their crash. Each day took more people down. Suicides became regular events. Hard working men were unemployed; fathers became hobos and *wetbrains*. Once-thriving businesses failed and families, with all their belongings, were tossed into the street.

Breadlines were everywhere. Efraym had stood on many of them; four abreast, lines snaking down the street, waiting for free food. Workers in flat caps and collarless shirts stood next to men in fedoras and bow ties. Feet shuffled along the pavement, faces frozen, empty bellies grumbling in gloomy symphony. Eyes focused on nothing as they inched down the line. It didn't matter what you wore or where you came from – if you stood near the front of the line you ate that day. If not, you went hungry. Efraym shook his head, trying to erase the picture.

The Irish kid on the stoop waved to a friend. They started to talk. Other boys joined them. Suddenly there were five angry, thirteen-year old kids with hungry eyes.

Efraym walked deeper into Irish turf. It was dangerous – and stupid – to challenge the lines. Jews and Italians watched out for each other. The others – Ukrainians, Greeks, and Germans were not so friendly. The Irish hated most of them.

What was a 45-year old man doing fathering a baby in these times? The city had changed dramatically during Efraym's lifetime. He was a Sephardic Jew; his family had lived in the city for nearly 300 years. New York was swamped with new immigrants at the turn of the century; it was a tongue-twisting chorus of languages while each group struggled to adapt.

The Ashkenazi Jews came from Eastern Europe, speaking mostly Yiddish. They fled the horrors of Christian Europe – pogroms, ghettoes, anti-Semitic laws, and poverty-stricken shtetls. They outnumbered the American Jews and Sephardim; Jews of Spanish descent lost their status.

The five Irish boys followed the Jew. Even though he was an old man in their eyes, he was on an Irish street where he didn't belong.

"What are you doing here, kike?" One snarled.

Efraym ignored him.

When Jimmy Walker was mayor of New York City, people called him *our gentleman Jimmy*. He was classy, dressed fancy, and a gift direct from Tammany Hall – more interested in pretty clothes and song writing than governing. He danced his way through the city, singing.

Will you love me in December as you do in May?
Will you love me in the good old fashioned way when my hair has all turned gray?

It was now December and Efraym's hair *was* gray. He wasn't singing or dancing. The stock market had crashed in '29 and the city waited for Walker to rescue them. It never happened.

The Irish boys snarled at Efraym.

Walker was a *gonif*, Yiddish for crook. In 1932 Judge Seabury finished him off. The mayor resigned and went on an 'extended vacation' in Europe. He was the first political exile Efraym had ever seen. No one missed the singing mayor.

Fiorello was next.

Fiorello LaGuardia was a tiny, brash guy who reformed the city and broke the stranglehold of Tammany Hall. He smashed gangster slot machines and built a famous airport in Queens. Everyone loved him. The man was half Jewish, half Italian – a matzah-pizza. Standing barely five feet tall, the people adored the tiny man known as "Little flower."

The Irish boys crept closer. Life held promise for the New York Jews until the 1930 crash of the Jewish-run *Bank of the United States*. America had no one to blame, so they turned to the Jews. The Jews were the cause of all evil – World War 1, bank crashes, the dust bowl, and The Great Depression.

Everything.

It was the same old story.

"*Goyim*," Efraym muttered, using Yiddish slang for non-Jews.

The Irish boys heard. "Kike," they shouted.

Efraym recalled what the Jews always said.

It doesn't matter who you become, what you do, where you go. As long as any part of you is Jewish, no one forgets. They will find you.

The Irish boys lunged.

Efraym tried to get away but he was too slow. They grabbed his shoulders, kicked behind his knees and in the small of his back. He collapsed on the street and the boys pounced. They beat his face and stomach with their fists. They kicked his ribs with their worn boots, shouted curses, and reveled in his blood.

The physical pain was awful but Efram welcomed it. Pain was a relief from the agonizing question about what was next.

The Irish boys loved it. "Harder," one yelled, smashing and breaking Efraym's nose. Efraym howled as the world darkened and he started to lose consciousness.

"No," a voice cried inside Efraym. "*Not now.*"

Efraym wasn't physically strong, especially against five young thugs, but he was smart.

"Run Isaac," he screamed through the blood pouring from his nose. "Down the alley."

The boys paused. "There's another Jew?"

Efraym yelled louder. "Run, Isaac, before they catch you."

The boys scanned the street. "Is there someone with you?"

Efraym howled as loud as he could. "Run now!"

There was one last kick in the ribs.

"Let's get the *other* kike!"

They scattered, racing down the street. Efraym was left behind, bloodied and broken.

I have to get home. Now.

Using all his remaining strength, Efraym scrambled to his feet and stumbled down the block in the opposite direction. He turned the right corners until he was back on Jewish turf. He found his apartment and scrambled up five flights of steps.

No one was home.

"Where are you?" he cried.

A neighbor, Mrs. McGrath, saw him. "The hospital," she said sternly. "Get there before the baby is born."

Efraym caught his breath. *The baby.* Their new life was about to begin.

With a bloody nose and cracked rib, Efraym ran to the hospital.

2

I was born marked for demolition.

The wind howled like feral cats. People clawed at empty bellies. In the old world they would have rushed to say prayers and incantations, but the evil eye was already upon us and everyone knew.

Stories, whispers, and horrors snaked through the icy city. Who wanted a baby? It was another mouth to feed – another struggle. My moment of birth was shadowed by a gruesome present. Where do you find hope in The Depression? Even a baby who could sense, but not make sense *of* the world she was entering, couldn't defy destiny.

Mother told me it was a grueling delivery. She labored for days. Her screams filled the air although she tried mightily to be brave. Father arrived at the hospital with blood on his clothes, a cracked rib, and broken nose. Mother didn't care – she was in too much pain.

The nurses wondered if Mother or I would survive such a violent trial. When the howling wind began, Mother believed it was the evil eye waiting to pluck away her only child. Mother, with her hazel eyes and flaming red hair, was not about to let that happen.

The doctor said it was because of her age. Mother was 38, Father was 45, both too old to have a baby. They had been married for 10 years. The day I was born no one cared but Mother and Father. I entered the world on the tails of The Great Depression and the eve of the most devastating war in human history. Instead of fairy tales about unicorns and princesses, my childhood would be filled with names like Auschwitz and Dachau, Hellcats and

Wildcats, and atomic bombs delivered by airplanes named *Little Boy* and *Fat Man*.

My first cries were shared with a score that resonated around the world – a radio broadcast by President Roosevelt. His voice crackled through the airways. Years later I would watch news reels of a grim-faced President and think, it's a fine birthday gift.

"December 7, 1941," the President said, is "a date which will live in infamy – the United States of America was suddenly and deliberately attacked by naval and air forces of the Empire of Japan."

Me and Pearl Harbor. We shared the date for my entire life.

3

Mother and I looked alike. We had red hair, hazel eyes, and dark skin that many found strange. Mother called it part Sephardic and something else – an undefinable mix that belonged to a long lost family secret.

Father and Hanya were different.

When I was older, I tried to teach my little sister to be silent like most children. It was impossible. I lived in Mother and Father's old values; Hanya was pure modern. She had brown hair and brown eyes, contrasting my wild, untamed mop of red. The separation between us was much deeper than our looks. Hanya was sharp; logic ruled her life. I was a dreamer, immersed in stories, histories, and ideas beyond what I saw every day.

I repeated the words that Hanya refused to accept.

It doesn't matter who you become, what you do, where you go. As long as any part of you is Jewish, no one forgets. They will find you.

"Wrong," Hanya would retort. "I don't believe you or Mother and Father."

Mother would wince in horror. "That's not the way a child speaks."

Hanya and I would look at Father to confirm or correct. Father always shook his head, a glimmer of pride dancing in his eyes.

"Say something," Mother would demand.

Father never said anything. I was Mother and Hanya was Father. He approved of her feistiness; her refusal to accept *they* as inevitable. People like Hanya would one day fight millions of Arabs to successfully insure Israel's future; challenge bitter racism to establish life-confirming civil rights; and resist people who believed in the genocide of all Jews.

People like me dreamed, held on to ancient stories, and assumed that our families and genealogy would insure our survival. Hanya never grasped who I was, and I never fully understood her.

"I believe in *gilgul*," I once confided to Hanya.

"What's gilgul?"

"The recycling of souls."

"I don't get it."

"*Gilgul neshamot* – the cycling of souls."

"Hebrew?"

"Yes."

"I don't speak Hebrew."

"It doesn't matter. Let me tell you the secret.

"I love secrets."

"The Early Kabbalists said that every soul is destined to return to heaven. If a soul hasn't worked things out on Earth, it can assume a new body and come back."

"I still don't get it."

I hugged Hanya. "Don't worry, some day you will."

Hanya shrugged. "There are too many things going on *now* to worry about old souls."

I ran my fingers through my red hair and sighed. "Just know that I have the sense. You might too, if you keep your mind open."

"What sense?"

"You'll feel it when you're ready."

Hanya would have to learn on her own. *They* were never far behind.

4

Mother and Father told us stories about the years before we were born. Anti-Semitism was rampant; we had to know what happened. The stories sounded more like old world blood libel than the city I loved. There were no Robin Hoods or brave princes to save the day; only people looking to hate.

"Jews made it through Black Tuesday," Mother explained, referring to the stock market crash in 1929. "The country was in terrible economic trouble but most Jews didn't have the money to invest in risky stocks. We saved and kept our dollars in the bank."

Father's face darkened and his eyes darted like an alley cat trying to hide.

"It was 1930," Mother whispered, "when we lost everything."

"The Jewish-owned Bank of United States failed," Father mumbled.

"Why was there a Jewish bank?" It didn't make sense to me.

Hanya looked bored, barely tolerating the old stories. Mother and Father glanced at one another. There was a profound anguish that I didn't understand.

Father took a deep breath. "I remember the day – December 11, 1930. Thousands of people lined Delancey Street in the lower east side. Everyone behaved even though rumors claimed that the largest New York retail bank was about to fail."

The name was Bank of United States.

Mother shook her head. "It was a rainy day; people held umbrellas and waved hand-made signs that made frightening demands. Many had the hand-printed messages: *Pay small depositors first. No evictions for non-payment of rent.*

We didn't understand what it meant – only that we were very scared."

"Three hundred million dollars *gone.*" Mother sighed. "Four hundred thousand depositors and sixty New York branches – mostly Jewish." Her voice trembled as if everything had been personally orchestrated by the devil.

Terrified families, frantic business owners, and crying children waited in front of the elegant facade of the Bank of United States. Long lines of traffic snaked past them. City noise fell on deaf ears. They were all in this together; at the same time each person, family, and business owner stood alone. A cold winter wind bit at their faces and their dreams as they waited uselessly.

It was one of the first bank runs in The Great Depression – followed by many others. Everyone wanted their money back. No one got it.

"We believed that the Bank of United States was different. It *had* to be different," Mother said wistfully. "It was run by Jews and staffed by Jews who couldn't get jobs in the banking community. Everyone thought that the bank had the full backing of the United States of America. How could America fail us?"

"It was just a bank," Father snapped. "They made it seem like it was protected by the power of America, but it wasn't. It was just a bank."

"And a scam. We trusted the bankers who used our money for bad real estate and stock deals. It was destined to fail."

"*They* said the Jews controlled finance around the world. That's some control."

They.

The silence lingered – dreams that would never be recovered.

They needed someone to blame. Rumors claimed that the Bank of United States wasn't bailed out because it was Jewish. Jews joined Catholics and immigrants as the target of hate for groups like the Ku Klux Klan, Silver Shirts, and German-American Bund. Henry Ford proclaimed, "I know who caused the war – the German-Jewish bankers! I have the evidence here. Facts!"

Evidence. Facts. *They* loved to blame the Jews. It was good sport like baseball, boxing, and horse racing. I looked at Mother and

Father and wondered how it could be their fault when they lost all their money but logic never figured in those things.

Hanya would nibble on a cookie as I absorbed every word.

"More," Hanya demanded.

Mother and Father thought she wanted more of the story. I knew better.

"Ssssh," I whispered. Even as a child, I knew that people needed their stories as much as they needed food and water.

Those years became part of me – a page in my legacy. "Kike" was burned into my vocabulary. Christ-killers? I didn't get it. I had trouble killing the cockroaches in our apartment. How could I have killed Christ?

Mother sighed. "They called us *Jew* York."

Father scowled. "FDR's plan was the *Jew* Deal."

Why would anyone hate me because I was Jewish? My best friend, Megan McGrath, was a Scot with blue eyes and blonde hair. We shared everything. She gave me a tiny cross and I gave her a hamsa. We traded words and secrets like *Tootsie Rolls*. The idea of hating her because she celebrated Christmas (which I secretly loved), and Mother lit candles on Friday night, was unimaginable. Megan *loved* Mother's dented brass candlesticks, purchased from a push cart and her old menorah. They were cheap because no one else had wanted them.

Megan thought they were magical.

"I wish my mother lit candles," she giggled.

It didn't make sense. If Megan saw magic in Shabbat and Hanukah candles, how could she hate us? How could *they* hate us?

5

We lived in East Tremont in the Bronx – an old-fashioned city neighborhood. The rules were simple. If there was no food for the Goldstein family next door, Mother would share what we had. When the widow Angelleti had to go to work, Mother watched her children. People sat on the stoops during hot, humid summers, laughing over the antics of children in the gutter. Mother also sat on the Southern Boulevard benches and cried with her friends about inattentive husbands, difficult children, and hard times. Father conferred with buddies in Crotona Park, arguing city and national politics. No one had money. We had each other; there was always a neighbor or friend to lighten our burdens. It was village life beneath the shadow of the great city.

The downtown politicians never understood.

"We're Jews," Mother said simply as if it explained everything. "People and the devil love to hate us. Right, Efraym?"

"Sephardic Jews," Father corrected her. "A minority within a minority."

"What does that have to do with the Bronx?"

"Here's what happened," Mother drilled us. "In September, 1654, shortly before the Jewish New Year, twenty-three refugees from Recife, Brazil arrived in New Amsterdam, tired and penniless." Mother sighed as if she had been one of them. "They were fleeing the Portuguese Inquisition and requested sanctuary from Director-General Peter Stuyvesant. He refused. The small group insisted that Stuyvesant contact the settlement's investors – the Dutch West India Company. The preacher, Killaen Van Sickles, backed Stuyvesant, writing letters to Holland, advocating against the Jews." She chuckled. "The Dutch West India Company was partly owned by the Jews in Amsterdam. Peter Stuyvesant and Van Sickles were told they had to let the Jews settle in New Amsterdam. We've been here ever since."

"*Before* the Irish," Father added.

"Peter Stuyvesant?" I persisted. "Not true. We learned about him in school and no one mentioned Jews from Brazil."

"Who cares?" Hanya frowned. "We're all New Yorkers *now.*"

Mother took us to see the ominous-looking statue in Stuyvesant Square Park – originally called Holland Square. "The land was donated by Peter Gerard Stuyvesant in 1836, one of the richest men in America at the time. The statue, created by Gertrude Vanderbilt Whitney, an ancestor of Peter Stuyvesant, was unveiled in 1941"

"The year I was born," I said quietly.

"Yes, Espie, the year you were born."

"No." Hanya scowled. "I don't believe it."

Mother laughed, tossing her red hair, eyes twinkling as if she owned the city. "Ask your teacher."

"There was one other story," Mother whispered, "that we tell in secret."

"What?" Hanya's eyes lit up.

"Some of our ancestors committed murder."

"No."

Mother nodded solemnly. "Centuries ago, there was an evil soldier who preyed on Jewish women."

"How?"

Mother lowered her voice. "He raped them."

Hanya and I were shocked that Mother used the word. All the girls in the Bronx *knew* what rape meant, but no one would use the word.

"What happened?" Hanya whispered.

"Our ancestor *killed* him."

"She was a hero?"

"Yes. Years later, when the Jews had settled in New Amsterdam, there was a lunatic who murdered many Jewish children. He had to be stopped and . . ."

"Another ancestor stopped him?" Hanya asked excitedly.

"Yes," Mother said soundly. "You can visit her grave in the old Jewish cemetery near Chinatown."

I shivered. Hanya clapped her hands.

"Does that mean we have a family legacy of murderers?" I asked quietly.

"Yes," Mother admitted. "Murderers and murdered . . . people chasing us . . ."

It sounded like an Ellery Queen mystery – intriguing, entertaining, but impossible.

Mother read my thoughts. "Did you know that Ellery Queen was a fictional character invented and written by two Jewish boys from Brooklyn – Daniel Nathan and Manford Lapofsky?"

"No way," I grumbled.

I was an adult before I discovered that Mother's stories were true.

6

Mother was determined to protect me. I grew up fueled by war, while Hanya only knew the post-war boom. Mother said that she named me Esperanza because it meant hope.

Esperanza was an ancient red-haired relative who survived King Ferdinand and Queen Isabella's expulsion of the Jews in 1492. There were a lot of Esperanzas in Mother's family. They all had red hair, hazel eyes, and wore *the* hamsa.

As a child, I dreamed of Esperanza – a Jewish Joan of Arc in a dark jungle, fraught with danger, leading people to safety in the name of God. I saw a wild, red-haired Esperanza battling a crowd of terrified people, her hands reaching out to a little girl guarded by soldiers and monks. Esperanza crying, her arms outstretched until a giant with armor and a red cross brutally knocked her to the ground. Esperanza, the murderess; Esperanza, the savior.

I never told Mother about the dreams.

"You were my first child, Espie," Mother explained. "God gave me a gift."

Mother thanked God every day. She was careful not to draw the attention of the evil eye. "I didn't want to make *it* jealous," she said quietly. "I was afraid it might take you away."

When I was born, she tied a red Kabbalah string around my wrist and hung hamsas throughout the apartment. One of my earliest memories was the large one on the wall near the crib. Other kids had cuddly stuffed animals while I had hamsas.

Most precious was the blue-and-silver hamsa that hung around Mother's neck. No one knew how old it was. It was passed down through the generations like a spirit selecting its owners.

One night when the sky was a musky blue, Mother sat on the stoop and told us yet another story. "My mother gave the hamsa to me."

I stared at the charm. The silver was crafted in delicate filigree with three uplifted fingers and two thumbs. An eye with a blue stone in the middle stared unblinkingly out at the world.

Hanya watched the kids playing in the street, barely listening.

"Hamsa is ancient," Mother whispered. "The word comes from the Aramaic. It means five."

"Five?"

Mother smiled. "Five – five fingers. A hand."

I stared into her eyes; they were bottomless, capturing time and courage that spanned millennia. "It keeps away the angel of death," she said softly. "Some say it's the hand of Miriam – the sister of Moses. Others believe it's the protective hand of God. It draws positive energy – life and happiness – and repels the evil eye."

"Is that why you have it on the wall?"

Mother nodded. "I hung a hamsa over the door when Father and I were married. I hung a hamsa in your room when you and Hanya were born. The one on my neck . . ." she paused. "The one on my neck is the most important. One day it will be yours, Espie; one day you'll pass it on to protect someone you love very much."

I reached out and touched the hamsa. My heart pounded and dizzying images swirled in my head.

"Yours, Esperanza," Mother repeated in a voice as ancient as the hamsa. "It will give you a good life." I looked into Mother's eyes and felt power surge beneath my fingers, as if it spoke to me.

7

The war was hard on Father. Like millions of Americans, he rushed to serve his country. He was refused – relegated to the "old man's draft" – men over forty-five, considered unable to fight. Mother cried in relief. While it probably saved his life, the old man's draft was a disgrace to him.

We lived in a two bedroom apartment that Father could barely afford. It was in a brick tenement that had turned gray after a half-century of city pollution. The front had a metal fire escape that zigzagged down five stories. A concrete stoop led to the entrance – steps that served as meeting ground, playground, and shared space. The street was narrow – few people owned cars; kids played punch ball and stick ball, marking off bases with chalk and sewer covers. Street vendors hawked their wares from pickles and used clothing to knife sharpening.

Everyone knew their neighbor's business.

"You can't sneeze without your neighbor blessing you," Mother laughed. She loved the small spaces and crowded streets. Sephardic Jews mixed with Ashkenazi. Litvaks and Galitzianers argued their superiority and both scorned the snooty Germans. We lived side-by-side in our small, crammed apartments with different traditions. Whether our families came from Turkey and Greece or Russia and Poland, it didn't matter. We were in it together – neighbors on streets where storekeepers greeted us by name and old ladies complained about the noisy kids in the gutter. In those days, the poor people were the richest in the city.

Father wasn't happy. He met with the other "old men" and railed at the government for not allowing them to fight. They volunteered for civil defense and promoted war bonds. Many landed lucrative jobs left open by the men who went to war.

Father got a civil defense job at Grumman Aircraft Engineering Corporation, way out on Long Island. The company was known for its "cats" – Navy fighter aircraft like *Wildcats* and *Hellcats*. Grumman was a major player in wartime production. Father was proud. He was making money and contributing to the war effort. He rose quickly in the mostly female ranks. By the time the war ended, he was a valued employee. That's when Father began to dream about getting out of the Bronx. It wasn't until Hanya was born in 1947 that his dream took on a new urgency.

8

Helen Jewett. Arnold Rothstein. Albert Anastasia. People loved to talk about murders. Murder, Inc. was a home-grown business. City gangsters became legends. We even had a few murderers in our family.

No one talked about Mother.

She was murdered by Robert Moses.

Mother's death was slow. It began after the official peace surrender signed on the *Missouri*. No one knew it was the beginning of our end. The post-war boom promised a rosy future. Soldiers came home and reclaimed jobs held by female wartime workers. People swarmed into New York looking for new lives. There was a housing crisis as the city struggled to deal with the swelling population. A father and two sons – the progeny of an Eastern European Rabbi – bought up potato fields on Long Island and built the prototype for a mass-produced suburban housing development.

They called it Levittown.

We flourished in East Tremont. Living costs were reasonable. Our neighborhood was middle to lower class – Jewish, Italian, German, Irish, Negroes, and Puerto Ricans. Families hung out at Crotona Park using tennis courts, baseball diamonds, basketball courts, and a *real* pond called Indian Lake. We were one mile from the Bronx Zoo, three miles from the Botanical Gardens, and crisscrossed by trains that could take us uptown or downtown. Chess and card games had been going on for 30 years. It was a good life. We were happy; Mother gave birth to Hanya and our small family was complete.

No one paid much attention to the rumors that drifted north from City Hall. Robert Moses wanted to tear up neighborhoods to build a road. It was crazy, like parting the Red Sea for traffic. Who needed a road when we had so much? Moses wanted to plow through neighborhoods that had been around for a hundred years. He didn't care that people lived there.

Father believed that Moses was the most innovative man in the city.

"He'll lead us out, like his namesake," Father promised Mother.

"I don't want to be lead anywhere," Mother said stubbornly. "I'm happy where we are."

Father was tired of the commute to Long Island. One day he came home excited – his face flushed and eyes twinkling. "It's true," Father cried. "I heard it from someone who *knows*."

"What's true?" Mother asked calmly.

"Robert Moses is going to tear down our neighborhood."

Mother looked at him with bored eyes. "They've been saying that for years."

"I know, but it's true *now*."

Mother shook her head stubbornly.

"You don't know what you're talking about."

"Of course I know. I *listen*."

Mother sighed. "You think you're such a big man."

"I *know*. Let me show you."

Father took us to a construction site in The South Bronx that looked like a bombed out city.

Hills of rubble were the only remains of many apartment buildings. Bulldozers and earth-moving machines crawled over the carcasses. The machine gun sound of jackhammers ricocheted through the air, backed by the concussion of exploding dynamite. In the middle was a river of gray-white road.

"Robert Moses," Father said happily. "This is his work."

"A Jew," Mother moaned. "What can you expect from a man who refuses to admit he's a Jew?"

Father shook his head. I gaped at the destruction. Hanya was too young to understand.

"He's evil," Mother said finally. "Robert Moses is evil. No conscience. No empathy. No remorse." Mother ran the words together like a column of numbers. "He has no *feeling*," she concluded.

"You're right, but he has money and power."

"He can't tear down East Tremont."

"He can and he will."

Mother was defiant. "I won't move."

"That's why," he pulled papers from his pocket, "I did this."

Mother froze.

"It's going to make you very happy."

A silence louder than the jackhammers filled the space between them. What was happening? I was ten years old; Hanya was six. It was 1951 and it felt like we were on the edge of a new war.

Father handed the papers to Mother. "That's why I did this," he repeated. "I bought one of the last houses in Levittown."

Mother's eyes were fire. "You did *what*?"

"I bought us a house. I thought it would make you and the girls happy."

"You bought a house *without* me?"

"I wanted to surprise you."

"You bought a house *without* me?"

"I'm the man of the family. I can do that."

Mother caught her breath. The fire in her eyes said it all. In that moment I saw the collapse of their marriage. How could things change so fast? How could Father have been so stupid? I knew the answer. If Father hadn't bought the house we would have remained in East Tremont; Mother would never have agreed to move. Father was forcing us to leave the Bronx.

"New house, new house," Hanya clapped her hands.

"I'm leaving," Mother said flatly.

"You can't. Don't you get it – they're going to tear down East Tremont."

They.

"You bought a house without me."

"I had to."

"You didn't have to do anything."

"You never would have agreed."

"I'm leaving."

"Mother!" I cried.

"You're a big girl, Espie. Father will take care of you and Hanya."

She left. Hanya cried for her mommy for three days. Father and I had no idea where she went. A friend's apartment? Crotona Park? The benches on Southern Boulevard?

We would never find out. When Mother returned her eyes were blank.

"We have to pack," she said in a monotone.

It was never the same between Mother and Father. A year later, long after we moved to Levittown, thousands of East Tremont residents received a letter signed by Robert Moses. It informed them that their homes were condemned to make room for the Cross Bronx Expressway. They had 90 days to leave. Less time than Ferdinand and Isabella gave to the expelled Jews in 1492.

9

One of Mother's friends, Lillian Edelstein, led a strike to stop the demolition, shift the road to the edge of Crotona Park, and save East Tremont. Robert Moses wasn't interested. Lillian would lose her apartment, along with her mother's unit, and sister's studio in the same building. Friends and neighbors were scattered. Our old building fell victim to the wrecking ball.

No one could stop Robert Moses.

Fiorello LaGuardia confessed, shortly before his death, that "Moses has too much power."

FDR said of Moses, "I don't trust him. I don't like him."

It didn't matter, Robert Moses explained. "You can draw any kind of picture you like on a clean slate and indulge your every whim in the wilderness in laying out a New Delhi, Canberra or Brasilia, but when you operate in an overbuilt metropolis, you have to hack your way with a meat ax."

Years later, in his Pulitzer Prize winning biography, Robert Caro said that philosophy never dictated Moses' action. He loved the power.

Father was right to get us out of East Tremont but Mother never forgave him.

Robert Moses reshaped the city and suburbs. He didn't care about the neighborhoods or people he destroyed. No conscience. No empathy. No remorse. Moses simply denounced the "common" people as "lousy, dirty and hostile."

Mother was one of them.

10

Mother and I hated Levittown. Father and Hanya loved it.

We moved into our bland new house. On the left side was a family with three boys. They were all slim with blue eyes and caramel-colored hair. The oldest boy had an icy, blank look like his father. They hated Jews. Words like "kike" were tossed behind my back. If I turned there were only smiles. I found swastikas scrawled in chalk on the sidewalk in front of my house. One day I found a drawing of a Nazi Iron Eagle in my mailbox. I screamed. Had *they* arrived at my front door?

Father told me to ignore them. This was America, not Germany.

On the right side of our home was a family with a new baby. I often heard the baby crying. Mother said that was normal for an infant. Maybe the baby was crying like me? Sad because she lived in Levittown and not the Bronx?

Across the street, a homely girl with curly brown hair lived with her family. Her name was Tamirah. She and Hanya were the same age and quickly became best friends. Both girls developed crushes on the handsome, icy-eyed boy who lived next door.

"I don't trust him," I warned Hanya.

"What does a Bronx girl know about Long Island boys?" She retorted.

Tamirah nicknamed him "Dutchboy" and followed him like an obedient puppy.

"Doesn't she *see*?" I asked Hanya.

"See what? He's sooooo cute."

I wondered how Hanya could be so blind.

"She's a true American," Mother suggested.

"Than what am I?"

Mother sighed. We both knew the answer. I was a mix of old and new, haunted by the possibility of *they* and imbued with something more . . . an intangible *sense* that Hanya didn't have, as if gilgul ran my life.

Levittown was the antithesis of what flourished inside Mother and me. The community was built on Long Island potato fields that had been decimated by a tiny creature with a pretty name – the golden nematode. The parasite was first found in Nassau County, Long Island in 1941, the year I was born. It bored into the roots of the potato plants and killed them before anyone knew what was happening. I thought that the golden nematode should be a princess not a parasite. I found a photo of the creature and instead of parasites, I saw tiny golden balls woven on royal red threads, like a tiny Christmas tree. How could such a pretty thing hurt so many plants?

Names and dreams rarely tell the whole story.

The farmers were eager to get rid of their infested potato fields. At the same time, there was a housing shortage and lot of post war dollars under the GI Bill. Young families wanted their piece of the American dream. Levitt & Sons entered the picture. The goal was to make a lot of very cheap houses. The Levitts bought the potato fields and got to work. They eliminated basements and garages from the blueprints, built on concrete slabs, and created a system of mass-producing homes. There were no middlemen or unions. They shipped in pre-cut lumber. Modern ranches sold for $7990; mortgages were extended to 30 years. Buyers put down a $90 deposit and paid $58 a month for their *private*, detached home. The houses measured 32 by 25 feet and came in five different exterior models. Interiors were identical; there was no garage, the attic was expandable, and appliances were included. Eventually a carport and 12-1/2 inch TV was added to sweeten the deal. The demand was overwhelming. Levitt & Sons claimed they completed one house every fifteen minutes. Nearly 18,000 homes were built in Levittown, Long Island. The town became the prototype for post war housing, joining the baby boom that was just taking hold.

Levittown was ugly. People lived in private boxes. I wondered what the golden nematode would have said.

"Where are the butchers," Mother cried, "the fruit stands and candy stores? Where are the stoops to sit and talk with my neighbors?"

Father ignored her. Hanya giggled.

People were polite but they weren't like my friends in East Tremont. Instead of Indian Lake we had scrawny saplings in front of each house. It was like living on a *Monopoly* game board. Jews and Catholics were reluctantly "permitted" but Negroes and Puerto Ricans banned. Years later, Peter Seeger recorded a song that said it best:

> *Little boxes on the hillside, little boxes all the same . . .*
> *they're all made out of ticky-tacky*
> *And they all look just the same.*

11

Father was now an American homeowner.

Mother and I mourned East Tremont. Within a few years, the neighborhood was gone, demolished by Robert Moses and his 'vision.' The Cross Bronx Expressway was an asphalt tombstone.

I made some friends in Levittown but they didn't have the Bronx edge. Few played chess and no one ever heard of punch ball. A suburban blandness pervaded the neighborhood.

Father and Hanya were happy. He was close to work and a loyal employee at Grumman. Hanya had Tamirah. They never noticed Mother's sadness. Father never saw that Mother didn't look at him in the same way. Their unconscious ballet was over; tandem shrugs and shared looks faded into the past. They rarely talked. I conveyed messages between them, filling the cavernous gulf in the small Levitt home.

Mother's health began to fail. That's when I brought her chocolate. It began with a game and evolved into a shared passion.

We collected and discussed our favorites, laughing a lot.

"Which do you like better, Espie, *Mounds* or *Almond Joy*?"

"How about a *Sky Bar* with caramel, vanilla, peanut and fudge fillings?"

"You're showing your age. A *Look!* bar with nougat, peanuts and chocolate is much finer."

"I would rather have *Whoppers* any day!"

Hanya thought our game was ridiculous. She preferred watching Dutchboy with Tamirah to sitting inside with Mother. For those few moments I saw life return to Mother's eyes as if we were back in East Tremont. The day Mother couldn't eat her *Junior Mints* I knew something was very wrong.

Father insisted on taking her to the doctor. Mother refused. She lost weight and her skin turned a gray-yellow color.

"I need you," I cried. "Please go to the doctor."

She finally agreed. The news was bad.

"She has pancreatic cancer," the doctor told us.

"What's that?" I asked.

Father never answered my question. I went to the library and learned it was the same cancer that had killed Mother's beloved Fiorello LaGuardia.

12

Mother accepted her approaching death with quiet dignity.

"Aren't you afraid?"

"No, Espie, I'm not." Her lips curled into a small, weak smile. "It's God's way."

"No. It's too soon."

"It is what it is."

I shook my head, terrified and confused. Mother grew withered, gaunt, and weak as the disease ravished her body. I brought chocolate every day because it was the only thing she ate.

One day, shortly before her death, Mother made me sit close to her on the bed.

"I have something for you Espie," she said weakly. Slowly, wincing from the exertion, Mother unclipped the silver hamsa from her neck. "It protected me all my life. Now it's your turn. Wear it because it will protect you. And when you're ready, give it to someone you love very much; someone who needs its protection."

"I can't."

"You have to – for me and all the Esperanzas before us – and all who will come after us."

Tearfully, I took the hamsa and hung it around my neck. "I love you," I choked.

Mother nodded. "I want you to look out for Hanya. She's so sure of herself – she doesn't understand the past like we do. Protect your sister because she'll need you to help her understand."

"Understand what?"

Mother touched the hamsa on my neck. "This."

"I don't get it."

"You do, Espie. Better than you realize. Follow your heart and trust your instincts. The hamsa will do the rest."

"That sounds . . ."

"Sssssh," Mother put her finger on my lips. "You'll understand sooner than you think."

"How do you know?"

"When you're so close to death you . . . see things."

"What things?"

Mother shook her head.

At that moment I realized for the first time in my life, I would have to go on without Mother. "Please don't leave me," I begged.

Mother hugged me weakly. "I'll always be with you."

13

I took Hanya to the city to prepare her for Mother's death. "Take Hanya to the cemetery," Mother advised. "It will help."

"Let's go on an adventure," I said to Hanya.

She looked at me suspiciously.

"I heard about a place in Chinatown – a tea parlor. It's supposed to be really great."

"You and me?"

"Just you and me."

"Can I bring Tamirah?"

"No."

"Why? You don't like her?"

"Of course I like her. This is a trip for sisters only."

Hanya agreed and we made plans. Father drove us to the Long Island Railroad station and we took the train into Penn Station in Manhattan, walked to Grand Central Station, and took the #6 subway downtown.

BROKEN BY EVIL

Canal Street was a buzz of activity – stores bursting with stuff like cheap souvenirs, Lucite, used junk, and hardware. The street was a gridlock of cars, trucks, and vans. More people crowded the sidewalks than all the residents of Levittown.

We made a right onto Mott Street and were amazed by the densely packed restaurants, shops, and signs in vertical Chinese letters. Scents drifted from the many restaurants, along with tiny bakery shops, grocery stores, and open-air fruit, vegetable, and fish markets. Hanya paused, trying to take in the scene. She gawked at the octopus, shivered at the eel, and stared wide-eyed at the dark eyes of strange-looking dead fish.

"Are you nervous?" I asked gently.

She laughed. "Nervous? I love the city. When I grow up I'm going to live here in a *huge* apartment."

I laughed with her. Hanya had such wild dreams. People moved *out* of the city to Long Island, not the other way around.

We followed Mott, paused to look into windows, read posted menus, and gazed at signs that advertised herbs, teas, and spices. We turned left on Pell and then right onto Doyers. Halfway down the tiny street we faced the oldest tea parlor in New York City, *Nom Wah.*

"Doyers Street is only one block long. It was named after Dutchman Hendrick Doyer who bought the property facing the Bowery in 1791," I began the story.

Hanya pretended not to be interested but she heard every word.

"He ran a distillery. A century later, the street was nicknamed the *Bloody Angle* for the notorious Chinese Tong Gang killers who favored the location. They used the sharp street angle and underground tunnels that connected the buildings for their "work." Hatchets were the choice of weapon, along with *snickersnees* – sword-like knives used as weapons. It led to the expression "hatchet man."

Hanya peeked around the turn in the street.

"Let's go."

We paused, facing the faded sign and old glass doors of Nom Wah.

"This is the best place in Chinatown," I added.

We opened the glass door and stepped inside the tea parlor – two Long Island kids on a crazy city adventure.

Nom Wah was a simple restaurant polished by time. We were the only non-Asians, fascinated by the unfamiliar tonal sounds of Chinese. There were red vinyl booths, yellow walls, and porcelain lucky cats. On the wall were autographed head shots of celebrities that neither of us recognized. We sat at a Formica table on cheap red chairs. The waiters came around with pizza-sized metal serving trays filled with dishes of tasty-looking Chinese food.

Hanya stared at everything.

"What do we do now?"

"Point," I said confidently.

We didn't know what we ate. We pointed to a dish that looked good and the waiter plopped it on the table.

"That's salt and pepper spare ribs," I smiled. "One of my favorites. Try this."

"I pointed to the shrimp and snow pea leaf dumplings. They're called *dim sum*," I explained, "translated as "little bit of heart." In the old days, travelers on the Silk Road and rural farmers would head to the local teahouse. It made for a very lively time."

Hanya stared at the unfamiliar food.

"Nom Wah opened as a bakery and tea parlor in 1920," I continued. "It's really famous – movies and TV shows have been filmed here."

Hanya was impressed. "It *looks* old."

We pointed and ate, and pointed some more. Each dish was better than the one before. Hanya and I ate until we couldn't touch another morsel. When we were finished, the waiter counted the plates and gave us a receipt in Chinese. I looked at the receipt as if I understood what I read.

"We have to talk," I said softly.

Hanya waited.

"Mother."

"I know."

"Know what?"

"Mother is going to die."

"How do you know?"

"I see more than you realize, Espie."

"I'm so sorry." I began to cry.

Hanya patted my hand. "We'll miss her, but it's the way of things."

"It shouldn't be."

She shrugged. "Father will take care of us. You're old enough to handle it."

"And you?"

"Father and you will take care of me."

"I don't know if I can live without Mother."

"Of course you can live without her. Especially with that." She pointed to the hamsa.

"You know?"

"I always knew it would go to you. You have the red hair and hazel eyes." Hanya spoke as if it was an irrefutable fact; something everyone took for granted.

I nodded. We were silent for a long time, thinking about our future.

"Mother wants us to go to the cemetery."

Hanya sighed. "Do we have to?"

"It's right here on St. James Place. They call it the Chatham Square Cemetery."

"OK, if that's what Mother wants."

14

Chatham Square Cemetery was the burial ground of the Sephardic Jews in New Amsterdam. It was originally much larger but now only a small remnant remained. Most of the bodies had been removed in 1855 by the city looking for more space. We walked down St. James Place and peered through a thick, iron fence mounted on a stone wall enclosing the graveyard. Towering buildings surrounded the old burial ground, their walls scarred and dirty. There were a few trees and bushes that struggled to guard the space. The cemetery was chained shut – no one could enter without permission. We read the plaque through the bars.

The First Cemetery
Of the
Spanish and Portuguese Synagogue
Shearith Israel
In the City of New York
1656-1833

The city faded. Sounds were muted as if we had stepped back in time. Someone or something spoke to us from the old graves. I knew that several of our ancestors were buried there – refugees who had sailed from Recife, Brazil and won sanctuary in Dutch New Amsterdam.

"She's buried here," Hanya whispered.

"Yes – the one who murdered the man who killed Jewish girls." I pointed to her headstone.

We stared at it.

"Do you hear that?" I asked softly.

Hanya shivered. "I think so."

A gentle voice drifted by us or *in* us, whispering as if she was telling us what to do next.

It's what you are destined to do – what God wants. Go and live well.

"Thank you," we said at the same time. Hanya and I were very different people but at that moment we were closer than we had ever been before.

I took Hanya's hand and we headed home.

15

Mother was rushed to the hospital the next morning.

A few days later she passed away.

She lay in the hospital bed, shriveled and lost in the sheets. I watched as the light ebbed from her eyes and her breath slowed – gasps punctuated by a silence that grew longer and longer. Mother took her final gulp of air and was still. She was gone. The nurses said that was what death looked like – breath slowly seeping from the body.

"The spirits are taking her home," one nurse said gently.

Father was in shock. Tears stained his face. He screamed; he grabbed her hands, her face, and her body.

"Nooooooo," he wailed. "Don't do this. Don't do this to *me*."

Hanya was silent, gripping the bedrail, her face a pasty white color.

I backed away, too stunned to comprehend. Do you ever really believe there's an end – even when you know someone is dying? The mind becomes desperate, clinging to the present as if it would last forever. It doesn't matter if the present is the process of dying. As long as it exists, as long as there is a single breath or heartbeat, there's hope. And that's me, Esperanza.

Hope.

I didn't cry. The pain was too pervasive; it invaded the core of my being. Everyone said I should cry. It would make me feel better. Feel better? I had to let go of Mother – I had to know that she was in a gentler place before I could move forward without her.

16

The funeral was dark and poorly attended. Mother had lost touch with most of her East Tremont friends. They were scattered throughout the Bronx and the rest of the city, probably reliving the days when we were together and cursing Robert Moses. Father's friends hardly knew us. They paid their respects with downcast eyes, wanting to be anywhere but talking to Father, me, or Hanya. Our family was small and scattered. A few relatives showed up from a sense of responsibility rather than fondness. I knew their faces and their names but none were a part of my life. Who cared? Mother was gone. Perhaps they were making a deposit on their own funeral so we would have to return the favor?

The Levittown neighbor on our right now had three children. They enjoyed Mother's old-fashioned ideas.

"We'll miss her," the mother said.

I believed her. It was nice to know that someone else would miss Mother.

The neighbor on our left came with the three boys. They were tall, thin adolescents. The oldest one, Dutchboy, was only a few years beyond me. He scared me. When I glanced at him he looked like he was smiling. I thought of Mother's indictment of Robert Moses.

He has no feeling.

I shivered.

Tamirah and Hanya held hands and stared at Dutchboy. I saw a leer on his face, like a stalking wolf. I averted my eyes as he approached them. He hugged them too tightly. Tamirah grinned.

"It's a funeral," I hissed, grabbing Hanya's hand.

He glared at me and said nothing.

The funeral was in *Gutterman's*, a building filled with dimly-lit rooms, noise-deadening carpets, and the smell of death mingling with flowery perfumes. Everyone spoke in whispers, whether they were attending Mother's funeral or the one next door. The chairs, mostly empty, were evenly placed in rows and the coffin set at the front for viewing. A man dressed in a black suit that screamed choreographed sympathy, invited us to visit the 'deceased.' He led us to Mother where she was lying, stretched out in a traditional pine box coffin. He backed off.

"Privacy," he mumbled.

It wasn't Mother; it was a waxy facsimile of what she had once been. Her face, gaunt from cancer, was puffed and painted to make her look better than real life. The make-up was thick and pasty. Mother hated makeup. Her dress, a favorite blue shirtwaist, was only half-visible. It was unbearable – a lifeless mannequin of the Mother I loved. The silver hamsa throbbed on my neck. Taking a deep breath, I retrieved a *Look!* bar and *Almond Joy* from my pocket. I could hear her voice.

Which do you like better, Espie – Look! or Almond Joy?

The Sky Bar *is the best – caramel, vanilla, peanut, and fudge fillings. Save the Almond Joy for last.*

Why did you have to die Mother? What will I do? What's next?

Gently, I placed the *Look!* bar and *Almond Joy* inside the coffin. Mother would be buried with chocolate.

"Are you crazy?" Hanya whispered.

In one of his rare moments of understanding, Father whispered beneath his tears. "Let her be, Hanya."

Tamirah stood behind us, watching and waiting.

I was sixteen years old. How could I face the rest of my life without Mother? How could I find a husband, have children, live a life? How could I leave her in this awful box, sunk in the ground, with only a few bits of chocolate and no hamsa? Why God? Why did you do this to me?

Words slipped gently into my thoughts as if directed by Mother.

I have something for you Espie. It protected me all my life. But now it's my time. Wear it because it will protect you. And when it's your time give it to someone you love very much; someone who needs its protection.

I'll always be with you.

The hamsa answered my questions. I had to go on because that's what Mother wanted. I turned from Mother and her coffin. Hanya backed away. Father remained. He couldn't stop looking and crying.

17

We buried Mother in a sprawling, crowded cemetery where her memory was crammed next to thousands of others who passed away; eternity in an assembly line of death. We did everything right. We sat Shiva, said the Mourners Kaddish, and did what was required of a Jewish family. It didn't change the pain.

I bought *Almond Joy* and *Sky* bars and ate them in hope that Mother would contact me from the diaphanous other side.

Tell me you're ok. Give me a sign, an omen, to know that you found peace. Maybe you're back in East Tremont sitting on the stoop . . .

Perhaps I heard too many stories – spirits and the other side, parallel universes, life after death. It bombarded my thoughts in a crazy, uncontrolled assault. I needed desperately to hope – to believe – but the chocolate tasted like ash and I never heard from Mother. Each morning I woke, dreaming about her so lucidly that for the first few moments I had to remind myself that she was dead; recall the cancer, her words, touch the hamsa on my neck, and hear the clods of dirt tossed on her coffin.

The light in Father's eyes died. Although they had grown apart since our move to Levittown, his soul went back to Mother and their earlier years. He made trips to her gravesite and the Cross Bronx Expressway. He tried to wrench the past back as if something was irretrievably stolen. He talked of The Great Depression, the day the wind howled like feral cats and I was born – along with FDR's telling the world about Pearl Harbor. Father held on to those years for the rest of his life. He didn't see my grief; instead he hung his heartache like a Purple Heart on his soul.

Father clung to Hanya, leaving me outside their circle of grief. I accepted it like I accepted the hamsa. It was my role and my duty in this life.

We didn't remove Mother's stuff from the house. Her clothes hung in the closet and her toothbrush remained in the bathroom. Her favorite mug sat untouched on the kitchen counter. Her slippers lingered uselessly by her bed, her coats hung lifelessly next to ours. Father made no excuses. He stared at the silver hamsa around my neck but never said anything. Instead, he rubbed his chin, allowed the sadness to fill his eyes, and turned away so I couldn't see his tears.

Father and Hanya buried themselves in the senseless voices, canned laughter, and vaporous comedy on the twelve-and-a-half inch TV that Levitt & Sons had given away with the last houses sold in Levittown. The tiny screen was their sedative.

I started walking the streets – the bare, ugly streets of Levittown where the ticky-tacky houses mocked me. I preferred the night when the street lights left deep shadows and I could melt into the dark. It made me feel better – concealed in an empty world where I was alone to tackle each day without Mother. They were long, lonely nights when my soul ached and the East Tremont street noise haunted my dreams.

It was on one of those nights when I took the walk that would change my life forever. I hoped that Mother would see me and say something.

I'm alright, Espie. Go on with your life.

Would I recognize her voice? I was already having trouble recalling the sound of her words as if she was slowly withdrawing from memory.

"I'm going out," I said to Father and Hanya. Their eyes were focused on the TV. No one worried.

If nothing else, Levittown was safe.

18

I shuffled down the front door path to the street. It was dark. The stars were gone. There was no sign from Mother. Nothing but an eerie suburban silence and a crescent moon that hung, like an ornament above scant tree tops.

"Please Mother talk to me," I cried out loud.

There was a snort behind me. "She's not talking to anyone."

I turned, startled. It was Dutchboy.

"She's not talking to anyone," he repeated, laughing.

I had a strange feeling that he had been waiting for me. Mother's description of Robert Moses popped into my head.

Evil. No conscience. No empathy. No remorse. No feelings.

"You're lucky," he chuckled. "Now that your mother is dead you only have to answer to your father and he doesn't give a shit."

I gasped. It felt like he punched me in my stomach. "Don't say that."

"Why? It's funny."

"It's not funny," my cheeks were hot. "It's not funny at all." I touched the hamsa on my neck.

His eyes followed.

"It *is* funny. Like your sister and her slut friend, Tamirah. The kikes who call me Dutchboy." He shrugged. "Do you know why they call me that?"

"No."

"Because my cock is big enough to fill the hole in the dam."

I shuddered.

"You know how I make the little slut happy? I let her suck me off."

"What? She's only a kid . . ."

He shrugged. "A kike like you. She's not good but I'm teaching her."

I clenched the hamsa.

"What ya got there Espie?"

"Nothing."

"It's not nothing."

He circled me. I stepped back, deeper into the shadow between our houses.

"A hamsa," he said lightly. "Isn't that supposed to protect a kike against bad stuff?"

"Shut up!"

He reached out and touched the silver.

"Get your hands off me!"

An evil grin curled his lips. Suddenly I was afraid – of the dark, of Mother not here, and of him.

"You know," he crept closer. "You come from murderers. Kike murderers who killed *my* people. That's not a good thing."

He pressed against me, his face inches from mine.

I tried to push him away but Dutchboy was like a boulder in the park. Unflinching.

"You know I wanted you since the first moment I saw you," his breath was hot against my cheek. "Your beauty outside only matches your beauty inside. You make me dizzy with desire."

He sounded like he was reciting lines from a soap opera.

"I'm going home."

He blocked me.

"I'm going home," I said again.

"You're not going anywhere, Espie. And when I finish with you . . ."

I froze.

He grabbed me, covering my mouth. I tried to scream but he pinned me against the wall of the house. I fought but he was too strong – I was helpless against him.

"I'm going to fuck you," he said lightly.

I used all my strength but his legs trapped me. He snapped my arms behind my back.

"Fight me, Espie, and I'll kill you."

I struggled wildly.

He slapped me across the face. "Whore," he cried gleefully.

He grabbed my throat.

"Fight me and I'll kill you." He said again, tightening his grip. I couldn't breathe. Was this what Mother felt like before she died?

"I'll let go if you stop – if you calm down. I'm going to fuck you either way. If you want to live just settle down."

Somewhere in the distance I heard voices from another television. He rubbed his groin on my belly so I could feel his erection. I couldn't move – I was rigid with fear. I bit his neck and drew blood but he didn't care. Panic rose, uncontrolled. Was this your sign Mother? Getting raped? I closed my eyes and prayed that it would be over quickly.

"I'm going to fuck you like you've never been fucked before. And when I finish, you know what you're going to say? Thank you. Thank you. Thank you." He laughed maniacally.

Mother. Help me.

"Before I give you the ride of your life, I'm taking this kike charm off your neck. It's in my way." He grabbed the hamsa, snapped the chain and tossed it on the ground. "No one will protect you now."

He yanked up my skirt and ripped off my panties. Then he unzipped his pants and pressed his raw, hard penis against my thigh. In a flash, thousands of years of rapes, massacres, pogroms, and the Holocaust flashed in my head.

It doesn't matter who you become, what you do, where you go. As long as any part of you is Jewish, no one forgets. They *will find you.*

Mother. Where are you?

I went limp, collapsing against the weight of my Karma.

"I'll show you what's good." Dutchboy panted, forcing apart my legs.

A sound, like a raging mastiff, pierced the air. Huge hands grabbed his shoulders and pulled him off me – hands that seemed to float detached in the shadows. The hands took his body and flung it on the ground, his penis flapping uselessly against his leg. He screamed like a feral cat. Feet kicked him, generating howls of pain. I remained frozen against the wall. I could only listen and taste the terror in my mouth. Finally Dutchboy lay still.

"Get the fuck away," a different voice said.

Dutchboy's hair was matted with blood. He scrambled onto his feet, shoved his penis into his pants, and glared at me.

"I'll be back, Espie," he hissed, "to settle our score."

"Move!" the other voice ordered.

And he was gone.

The voice belonged to a man nearly ten years older than me. "Are you okay?" he asked softly.

I nodded.

He had brown eyes and curly brown hair, a large Jewish nose, and empathy in his face. He turned his back to me. "Cover yourself."

I grabbed my torn panties and smoothed the skirt over my nakedness.

He bent down and picked up something.

"My name is Eli," he added. "You're safe now." He took my hand and put something in the palm. Then he closed my fingers. "I think you need this." He paused. "I'm going to walk you home now and wait outside until your door is locked."

I couldn't speak.

He took my arm and gently led me to my front door.

"Go," Eli said softly.

I opened the door and stumbled inside. Eli backed away. I locked the door and opened my hand. Eli had rescued Mother's hamsa. I started to cry – thick, choking sobs that shook my entire body. Father heard and rushed over, wrapping his arms around me.

"Cry, Espie," Father said. "It's about time you let out your tears for Mother."

I looked over Father's shoulder and out the window. Eli nodded. He mouthed one word.

Safe.

He turned and walked away. I watched until he faded from view.

That's when I knew.

Mother had sent me Eli. He would be part of me for the rest of my life.

19

Mother never returned after she sent Eli.

Eli and I didn't speak of that night again. Dutchboy disappeared. Later, Hanya and Tamirah tearfully informed me that he was sent away to school. I never told them what happened. In fact, I never told *anyone*. I thought it was my secret.

Dutchboy went to a Christian school where Jews were not allowed. When I saw his brothers on the block they averted their eyes as if they *knew*. How could they? It had been me, Dutchboy, and Eli. Perhaps their brother bragged?

I looked at Tamirah and felt sorry for *her*. Dutchboy had manipulated her into sex; controlling her at a young age. What would the future hold for the sharp, witty kid so fluent in numbers? Would she be tainted like me? I tried very hard to befriend her; become an older sister who *cared*. Hanya was jealous but I ignored it. Tamirah needed a role model.

Mother's lasting gift, Eli, grew to be one of the greatest joys in my life.

Eli gave me time to recover. He would show up with small gifts of chocolate. We spent more time together. He taught me how to laugh again; how to see hope. We became close, sneaking kisses. One day he brought me chocolates from *La Marquise de Presles*, a confectionary boutique in Paris. It was owned by Robert Linxe, the man who later started *La Maison du Chocolat*. Tucked beneath the chocolate was an engagement ring. Mother would have loved the chocolate *and* the ring. It was better than anything I had ever tasted.

Eli and I built a life together. We married after I graduated high school – a small ceremony in the Rabbi's study. Eli worked in the city as a business manager and made a good salary. We bought a small, two-story house on Long Island and had our first daughter, Aldi. Beth came next. Our family was complete.

I immersed myself in caring for my family and home. Ironically, neither Aldi nor Beth had the red hair and hazel eyes that Mother and I shared. I wondered if there would ever be another Esperanza to receive the hamsa.

Many years later, I saw Dutchboy on TV. He was running for U.S. Senator. Eli and I were amazed that an attempted rapist could campaign for public office. No one seemed to know, or care about who he was. We assumed that the truth would come out, as it usually does in politics.

It never happened.

Instead, Dutchboy became New York's favorite son and won by a landslide.

Eli and I sat in our home watching the election returns. Dutchboy's words reverberated in my mind like ball smashing wildly against the unflinching brick walls.

I'm going to fuck you like you've never been fucked before. And when I finish, you know what you're going to say? Thank you. Thank you. Thank you.

"Thank you. Thank you. Thank you," The new Senator began his acceptance speech. I clutched my hamsa.

Aldi and Cal

1

It was too quiet.

Aldi shivered. Living with Joshua taught her that *too quiet* could be lethal. She sat at the kitchen table and clutched a cup of tea. After nearly seven years of parenting, the beautiful eight-year old boy had shattered her illusions. Aldi's faith in herself as a mother had been destroyed and her marriage had been brought to its knees.

Yet she loved Joshua more than her own life.

2

Aldi and Cal were infertile. They endured years of unsuccessful fertility treatments, finally deciding to adopt a baby. They faced another obstacle – open adoption. In the new approach, the birth mothers *chose* who would adopt their babies; making decisions from portfolios and DBM [Dear Birth Mother] letters. With Aldi and Cal's training, intellect, and not-too-good looks, young pregnant girls found them unappealing. Aldi and Cal fell to the bottom of the lists.

Aldi was a university administrator and Cal was an ex-professor who traded his lectern for *Tree of Life,* a rare and antiquarian bookstore. They lived in a large brick Gothic-style house with white trim, mysterious peaks, turrets, and windows in Smithville, Long Island. Aldi loved her quirky house – its different look was perfect for her and Cal.

They were walking distance to Walden Pond, a small fishing pond and park once used by the Merokee Indians before the settlers came from New Amsterdam. It was a beautiful, peaceful spot in the middle of the suburbs; scarred only by leftover beer cans and condoms from the local teenagers. Aldi and Cal ignored the artifacts of adolescence. Instead, they followed different trails around the park, weaving in and out from the pond shore, peeking through the brush at noisy Canadian Geese, nonchalant Long Island ducks, or sea gulls that loved to disrupt the balance.

One of their favorite pastimes was to follow a dirt trail that led to a flat rock overlooking a pool formed by the pond. Aldi and Cal would sit on the rock, hold hands, and watch the whirlpools and reflections in the water. They spoke about life and transcendentalism, touching on subjects as dizzying as the pool at their feet.

Eventually, transcendentalism morphed into another subject – Aldi was desperate for a child. They only had one remaining option – foster care. Aldi convinced Cal to foster a fifteen-month old child named Joshua. Kiran, the social worker from the Department of Child and Family Services, had told them that little Joshua had problems.

Joshua doesn't like to be touched. He's removed from other people. He's very calm, as long as you leave him alone. He doesn't seem to notice when there are other kids around. As an infant, he didn't suck well so he was a difficult baby to feed. When he got older, he wouldn't allow anyone to hug him. He's built a cocoon around himself as if afraid that he's going to be abandoned again. Some people call it RAD – *reactive attachment disorder – a result of his birth mother abandoning him.*

Joshua was a Safe Haven baby. His birthparents dropped him off at a police station on the day he was born. By doing so, the law protects the birthparents from any responsibility for their child – they left no name, medical history, or forwarding information. The newborn was clean and healthy in the hospital. There were no signs of prenatal exposure to drugs or alcohol and no indication of physical abuse. He spent a week in the hospital because he began to cry and thrash without stopping. The nurses said he was angry. The doctors searched for medical reasons. Nothing was found. One day he stopped. He was quiet. The neonatologist declared him ready, reporting no physical or mental reason to preclude placement and eventually, adoption. They noted that Joshua would thrive in a warm, healthy home.

Joshua came with a note – a crumpled napkin pinned to a scrap of red checked tablecloth.

> *Please give my baby a safe haven.*
> *His name is Joshua.*
> *I love him. I hope he*
> *Has a better life than me.*
> *Goodbye.*
> *Joshua's Momma.*

Aldi and Cal tried to make sense of what it all meant. Was the man who brought Joshua to the police his father, grandfather, or no relation? The police reported that an aging biker with tattoos delivered the baby and refused to answer questions. They had to accept the baby and the man's silence. It was the law.

Aldi, and her reluctant husband Cal, accepted the silence like a *tabula rasa* – blank slate. Joshua came with no history.

Joshua's file told the story of two foster placements before moving in with Aldi and Cal. Both placements were troubled. Aldi's sister, Beth, suggested that they remain permanent foster parents so if anything went wrong, Joshua could be returned to the system. Cal said little, putting locks on his home office and spending longer hours at *Tree of Life*.

Aldi's Mom, Espie, was cautious. "I hope you know what you're doing. Dad and I will support you either way."

Aldi was defiant. In the end, she convinced her entire family that Joshua was meant to be their son. She and Cal adopted the child. Years passed with heart-wrenching secrets kept by Aldi.

No one knew the *real* Joshua.

3

Once Aldi tried to admit the truth to Mom. They were sitting at the table in the kitchen. Aldi steeped a pot of *Chai de Chocolat* tea. Joshua was napping and Cal was at *Tree of Life*. Mom knew that Aldi was having a tough time.

"You look tired," Espie said softly.

Aldi shook her head. A single tear made its way down her face. Angrily, Aldi swiped it away.

"He's very difficult."

"Cal?" Mom asked hopefully. She stared into her tea. Her face was soft and gently wrinkled; her red hair streaked with gray because she stubbornly refused to use hair dye. "Talk to me."

Aldi wanted to say that her son was perfect; the three of them were like the happy families on TV. The words wouldn't come. Her shoulders sagged. "He's so . . ." Aldi didn't know what to say. "You know, God, karma and the cosmic forces believed I would be a bad mother so I was infertile. I didn't believe them. I just laughed and said, *watch me.*"

Aldi sipped her tea and closed her eyes as if she could rewrite her life. When she opened her eyes and looked at Mom there was no place to hide.

"Those same forces responded," Aldi tried unsuccessfully to joke. "They said watch who I send you."

"No child can be that bad," Mom lied. "You and Cal . . . you're still learning. You'll figure it out."

Yeah, sure.

"Maybe you should get professional help."

Aldi froze.

"It couldn't hurt. Beth and I talked about it and we agreed that it would be a good idea . . ."

"You and Beth *talked* about it? Behind my back?"

Beth, Aldi's sister, was the perfect daughter, mother, and wife. It was no surprise that she had two perfect little girls, Sage and Danielle. Sage even had her grandmother's red hair and hazel eyes.

Aldi hated and loved Beth's good fortune.

"It wasn't like that. We were just talking and . . ."

"It wasn't like that? Then what was it like?"

Mom looked away.

"Joshua will be just fine," Aldi retorted.

It was a lie.

Now, the house was too quiet.

Aldi shivered. *Too quiet* was dangerous.

4

Aldi knew that Joshua would never be *just fine*. That morning she found a dead, dissected squirrel on the front lawn. Road kill? Feral cat? She closed her eyes, held her breath, and picked up the remains, stumbling through the grass to the trash. She dropped the pieces in the can and covered them with leaves so Cal wouldn't find them.

It wasn't the first time.

The truth was difficult to grasp. Aldi failed. She loved a kid who constantly rejected her. If he needed comfort, she would open her arms and he would come running – only to fall on the floor, curled in a fetal position, and refusing her touch. If she reached for him he would howl.

Aldi couldn't penetrate his cocoon. She craved for three words that Joshua refused to say.

I love you.

Aldi said the words in her head. She said the words out loud. She said them to Joshua trying to convince him. There was no response and no interest. How could she tell Mom that she and

Cal were terrified; Joshua had held them hostage since the day he moved into their Gothic home? How could she explain the lingering grief for the child she aborted years ago?

If I had that baby, I wouldn't have Joshua.

She hated the memories kept secret inside herself. Aldi had a brief affair with the infamous Senator. Cal was recovering from the tragic death of his parents and brother in a car accident. She was lonely and The Senator approached her, late at night, in her empty office.

He was fiercely good-looking in the dim light; tall, with a deep voice, teasing smile, and sultry eyes. He moved in an aristocratic grace, tossing his thinning, caramel-colored hair as he held his head high, squared his shoulders, and spoke in an arrogant, compelling voice. Although he was twenty-seven years older than Aldi, he seemed younger than Cal. He came into her office and closed the door behind him.

Aldi, he whispered, caressing her name. Aldi. I've wanted you since the first moment I saw you. Your beauty outside only matches your beauty inside – you make me dizzy with desire. I dream about holding your body, naked, against me. Making love . . .

He came to her office every other night for one month.

"Do you know," he said pleasantly, "that the kikes call me Dutchboy because my cock is big enough to fill the hole in the dam?

She ignored his words. She also ignored the times he got rough, plunging into her without foreplay, hissing in her ear.

I'm going to fuck you kike, like you've never been fucked before.

He twisted her arms and bit her breasts, grabbed her wrists, and pounded her body. She was scared; it hurt and was crazy exciting at the same time. Other times he would thrust his penis into her mouth, leaving a sticky trail on her tongue.

Aldi screamed and cried. She was hungry and fevered, enveloped in his dark soul. When he was finished, he smiled. It was the most beautiful smile in the world, paired with his signature words.

Thank you. Thank you. Thank you.

He returned to Washington. When Aldi discovered she was pregnant, she tried to contact him. The Senator's aids surrounded him like gladiators, never allowing access.

Aldi had no choice. If she had the baby she would lose Cal. If she aborted the baby, life would continue, her secret secure. Medically, everything went smoothly. Psychologically, God, karma, or some cosmic power was punishing her for betraying her husband. She and Cal were infertile.

Joshua entered their lives. They adopted him – a child with no history.

Was the boy a curse or a blessing?

Worst of all, The Senator *knew.* He went to Cal's store and gave them a gift – the story of a local pizzeria owner who was murdered on the same day Joshua was born. Enraged, Aldi rushed to The Senator's office. He was calm, bemused. The Senator threatened to expose everything; Aldi would lose what he nicknamed the *demon boy.* There was only one way he would keep her secret.

"Do me," The Senator demanded, "or I'll tell everyone."

Aldi loved Joshua more than her own life. She would do anything to keep him.

5

Aldi thought about the abortion when she found Joshua sitting on the floor, banging his head against the wall . . . and smiling. Aldi thought about The Senator's name for the child, *demon boy,* when she struggled to stop Joshua from kicking, screaming, biting, and doing anything to keep her away. Aldi refused to give up. Instead, she lied using excuses to explain her bruises. Cal listened with doubt embedded in his eyes.

I tripped on the stairs.

I fell in the kitchen.

You know those rocks in the garden . . . ?

Cal didn't believe her but he never asked questions.

It became apparent as the years slipped by; Cal didn't want to know. Aldi prayed that one day Joshua would change, smile, and whisper, "I love you mommy."

It never happened.

Aldi was determined never to give up on her son.

She had to attend to *now* and it was too quiet. Way too quiet. She placed her half-filled cup of tea on the granite countertop. It was fine Earl Grey Cream, straight out of London. Aldi remembered the time Joshua had poured an entire jar of pepper into her tea canister, mixed it, and waited.

"Why would you do something like that?" Cal had asked.

"I wanted to see what happen," Joshua grinned.

"You hurt mommy," Cal said to the sound of Aldi gagging.

Joshua shrugged. "It is a boring day. Now it won't be."

Aldi struggled out of the bathroom to defend Joshua. "He didn't do it on purpose."

"Of course he did it on purpose."

Joshua hid behind Aldi and grinned at his father.

It had been awful. The tea burned Aldi's mouth and throat – she coughed, sputtered and ran to the bathroom for hours. She grabbed for water but that made it worse. Cal chased her with a slice of bread. She swallowed the bread, which deadened some of the burn. And Joshua?

Watching. Smiling.

That was the last time Cal tried to get involved. He retreated into the safety of *Tree of Life*. Joshua was so young. Cal suggested *returning* Joshua but Aldi was horrified. How do you return a child? Your son?

It wasn't *legally* or *morally* possible.

Aldi knew Joshua was troubled since the first day they met at the Department of Social Services. No normal kid smashed toy cars against the wall for fun, watching them break and shatter while horrifying adults. Even Sharon Candido, his foster mother at the time, had shock in her eyes. Everything since that moment drove home the fact that the child Aldi loved was broken.

And I'm not good enough to fix him.

She sighed. It was definitely too quiet.

Aldi slipped off the kitchen stool and headed for the stairs. Joshua's playroom was in the light-filled turret on the second story. Slowly, she climbed the elegant wood risers, clutching the heavy oak handrail. The sage carpet runner was soft beneath her feet. Suddenly there was a blood-curdling howl that felt like a knife plunging into her breast.

Aldi ran.

She reached the top of the stairs, her heart pounding, and rushed into the turret playroom. Joshua wasn't there. She heard the howl again. Now it was familiar. A few days ago, Beth had given them a kitten. Cal immediately fell in love and named her Illusion.

Joshua didn't like his father favoring the kitten.

There was another primal feline cry. It came from the bathroom. Aldi froze.

She wanted to drift into another world where Joshua played Little League and was class president. Instead, she crept to the closed bathroom door and listened. Joshua was humming an odd, wordless tune. Aldi had never heard it before. His voice was high and sweet – he sounded angelic. *Normal.* Aldi closed her eyes and took a deep breath.

She opened the door.

Joshua was staring into the toilet bowl. "Hi Mommy," he said cheerfully.

The bathroom tiles were streaked with blood. Shiny metal pushpins were scattered on the floor. Joshua had cat scratches on his arms and legs. He pointed to the toilet.

Illusion was covered with blood. Pushpins stuck out from all over her body. She was wedged in the toilet bowl, not moving.

Aldi caught her breath.

"I try to flush her down the toilet," Joshua explained, "but she wouldn't fit."

"She's dead," Aldi hissed, not believing her eyes. "Dead."

"So?"

Aldi screamed.

6

Cal surveyed *Tree of Life*. It was a special shop, treasured by many local people. He reveled in the leather-and-paper smell of old books. The walls were lined in dark shelves and the aisles were narrow, filled with tables stacked with books. In the corner there were glassed-in shelves where he displayed his most precious volumes: J.R.R. Tolkien's hardcover, first edition trilogy of *The Lord of the Rings* and J.D. Salinger's first edition of *The Catcher in the Rye*.

Cal rarely left the store. He arrived early in the morning to avoid Joshua's "wake up" temper tantrums, battles over food, and breaking things. Most days there was a wad of sheets in the hall from wetting the bed.

"Enuresis," Aldi explained.

Another testament to Joshua's troubles.

Whether it was a toy, favorite mug, eyeglasses or a collectible, Joshua loved smashing it into a thousand pieces. Aldi tried to correct him.

"Joshua that's not nice" or "Joshua did you really mean that?"

Joshua denied everything. Aldi praised him for things a normal kid should do, like washing his hands, not gleefully tearing worms in half, or crushing bugs with his fingers. She got that from television shrinks and parenting-the-difficult child books.

"I'm really proud of you Joshua – you didn't break anything."

"You did a great job at breakfast – you didn't break your plate or steal cookies."

"See Joshua, you don't need to wave a knife to get attention."

Cal shivered. Who would blame him for steering clear of the boy? Who would agree with Aldi's condemnation?

"You don't understand Joshua. He's a very hurt child."

"You need to love him more."

"You need to have patience."

The accusations rattled in his head. Some were true. Joshua was a hurt child *and* Cal wasn't sure how he felt about the kid. Joshua was tough to love; there was nothing soft or warm about him. It was all hard edges, anger, and those awful, flat eyes. Cal loved Aldi. But Joshua?

Inevitably, the story of St. William of Rochester crept into his thoughts. Cal rubbed his head as if trying to erase the Catholic Patron Saint of Adopted Children. Cal was Jewish; the story should have no meaning. Yet it gnawed at him – an ancient tale that wouldn't go away. He had first read about David in the plain black volume written in 1921, published by A&E Black, London.

The Book of Saints: A Dictionary of Servants of God Canonised by the Catholic Church: Extracted from the Roman & Other Martyrologies

The story haunted Cal.

William was a wild young man until he reached adulthood and devoted himself to God. He was a baker, and felt great empathy for poor and neglected children, donating every tenth loaf he baked. One day, on his way to mass, William found an abandoned baby. He named the baby David and adopted him.

Years later, William and David went on a pilgrimage to the Holy Land. They stopped to rest in Rochester, England. Suddenly, David turned on his adopted father – clubbed him, cut his throat, robbed the dead body, and fled. Because William was murdered on a holy journey, he was considered a martyr. After that, there were many miracles credited to his remains; in 1256 he was canonized by Pope Innocent IV.

Why would David murder the father who loved him? It made no sense; Jews didn't believe in that stuff anyway. He leaped back into the present and thought about Aldi's sister Beth who visited less often to avoid the storms; and Espie and Eli who were afraid of Joshua but reluctant to admit it. No one wanted to be around the kid or spend time in their house for too long.

Except Aldi.

Cal had searched for solutions online and in the same parenting books Aldi read. Nothing described Joshua. There were causes and effects, psychological jargon, and parenting strategies but none hit home. It confused him. After all, Joshua hadn't been born addicted, a crack or fetal alcohol syndrome baby, or raised in an institution. He didn't come from an Eastern European orphanage or a South

American country run by drug lords. His foster care placements were with reliable people; there was no abuse, neglect or trauma. What went wrong?

"Give him time," Aldi insisted. "Things will work out."

"How much time?"

"I don't know. I just know he needs it."

"It's not working out now."

"Time, Cal. That's all he needs. He'll grow out of this."

Cal doubted that time would change anything. If he could look into the future where a grown-up Joshua was okay; where he went to college and laughed like other kids; things might be different. Cal couldn't see past today.

He suggested consulting a professional. "I heard that Kiran left DSS and started a private practice. She always got along with Joshua."

Kiran was the social worker from DSS who had originally introduced them to Joshua.

He hadn't just "heard" – Cal called DSS after he saw Aldi's bruises. He located Kiran's private office, wrote down the number and address, and approached Aldi.

"I'm fine," Aldi said breathlessly. "Joshua is fine, too."

"I'm sure. But a little help won't hurt."

"I can figure this out."

"No one can figure this out."

"Time," Aldi mumbled. "Just give me time."

Cal let it drop. Aldi hadn't figured out anything in seven years. He kept Kiran's information in his wallet.

Just in case.

7

Cal left the store and crossed over to the tiny, unattached building that was his office. He entered and sat in the high-backed leather chair, behind his antique American roll top desk, and surveyed his domain. His desk was the best of its type, with raised side panels, tiny shelves, drawers, and slots. Cal vowed that he would clean it out one day but it remained stuffed with sticky notes, business cards, and other small bits of paper.

One wall of his office was devoted to the *Roycrofters*, a now little-known community of artists, craftsman and book makers in Aurora, N.Y. He stared at the photo of Elbert Hubbard, the Roycrofter founder. Cal felt a connect with Hubbard, who was born in 1856, the son of a country doctor and a teacher, and the grandson of a bookbinder.

At the height of his success, Elbert and his wife took a cruise on Cunard's flagship – the world's most elegant ocean liner, called *The Lusitania*. Cal could close his eyes and see bands playing, people partying, and gourmet food served in ornate dining halls. A German U-Boat lurked beneath the hazy sunshine above the Irish Channel. No one knew that danger was close.

Suddenly the first torpedo was shot, easily hitting its target. The second torpedo followed with an explosion that took out five thousand live artillery shells stored in the hold. The ship listed and rolled to its side; only half of the lifeboats could be launched. The *Lusitania*, along with twelve hundred people, sank in less than eighteen minutes in the attack that started World War I – *the war to end all wars*. Later, the Jews would be blamed for causing the war.

Cal recalled his favorite Elbert Hubbard quote:

Henry Thoreau strolled out of his cabin and looking up at the placid moon, murmured, "Moonshine, after all, is the only really permanent thing we possess."

Moonshine. He wondered if he, like Hubbard, would succumb to a sudden, unforeseeable death. Was *Tree of Life* another bit of moonshine? What force was steering his destiny? Perhaps there was another *Lusitania* lying in wait? It had been seven years of Joshua's unsmiling face, cold eyes, and bizarre behavior.

Was Joshua killing moonshine?

"Joshua will get better," Aldi insisted in her usual refrain. "I know it."

"How can you possibly know that?"

"I do. Call it instinct – a mother's instinct."

Nothing changed except for the days and years on the calendar.

Joshua didn't get better. He got worse – he cursed, wet his bed, and got into trouble at school. Everyone wanted to quiet the boy. It wasn't a surprise when Beth showed up with a tiny kitten. Perhaps a pet might mellow the boy? Beth's youngest daughter, Danielle, wanted to keep the kitten but her eldest, Sage, stroked the animal and stared at Joshua.

"Take good care of her," Sage said.

"Maybe it will soften him" Beth said too loudly.

Sage retrieved a bar of chocolate from her pocket. It was organic dark Belgium chocolate with blueberries and acai fruit. Sage loved her chocolate. She spent many afternoons with

Grandma Espie laying out their chocolate treasures, trading, laughing, and discussing exotic flavors. Cal didn't quite understand why, but he knew that Sage and his mother-in-law shared a special connect.

"It's her red hair," Aldi explained. "Mom got her red hair from her mother, who said it was in the family for hundreds of years. It skipped my generation and came out in Sage."

Cal wasn't surprised. Sage was everyone's favorite.

Sage gave Joshua a bar of chocolate along with the kitten. The chocolate was called *Nirvana*.

"Take good care of her. She's only a kitten."

Cal had his doubts. *Nothing* could soften Joshua. When he saw the boy cuddle the kitten there was a glimmer of hope. Cal didn't expect his own reaction when the kitten crawled in his lap. It was tiny, warm, and made little mewing sounds showing affection that Joshua couldn't.

Maybe this is the link that will transform Joshua?

There were lots of stories about life-changing animals. Cal thought of Lassie, Einstein, Fang and Toto. He thought of the Cheshire Cat, Birdie, Boris, and Marmaduke. Maybe a kitten would make the difference?

"Let's call her Illusion," Cal grinned mischievously.

Aldi frowned. Joshua sneered. The name stuck.

They kept the kitten. It slept in Joshua's room. Every night, Illusion left Joshua and curled up against Cal.

Joshua didn't like that.

Cal loved it.

Cal sighed. His cell phone rang and he pried it from his pants pocket. It was Aldi. He made the connect.

Aldi was hysterical.

What the hell are you saying?

8

Cal rushed home. He stared at the drowned corpse of Illusion. Aldi fell into Cal's arms, trembling, her face stained with tears, her voice hoarse from alternately sobbing and screaming.

Joshua watched them calmly.

"Why did you kill Illusion?" Cal demanded. "Why would you even *want* to kill the cat?"

Joshua tilted his head. "I didn't kill the cat," he said sweetly. "I never kill the cat. I love Illusion."

Aldi froze.

"Then who killed Illusion?" Cal roared.

"Mommy," said Joshua. "She never like Illusion."

"Mommy wouldn't do that."

"She did," Joshua smiled, lifting the dead animal from the toilet bowl. "See."

He held up Illusion and dropped the bloody corpse on the tile floor. It landed with a *splat* that made Cal shudder.

Aldi pulled away from Cal. "You said *I killed Illusion?*"

Joshua nodded. "Don't lie Mommy," he spoke in a voice that mimicked Aldi. "That's bad."

Aldi and Cal stared wide-eyed at their son.

"Illusion doesn't fit in the toilet. Let's throw her in the garbage or burn her in the fireplace. Yeah. It's fun to watch. You like that, Mommy. Burn the cat?"

Aldi and Cal were dumbfounded.

"And then," Joshua continued. "When Illusion is all burned up we can go for ice cream."

9

It took hours to scrub the bathroom and get rid of the blood. Cal found an old wicker basket and gently placed the kitten inside. He put the basket against a big, sprawling tree in the yard, laying it between the roots as if the tree was embracing the dead animal.

Cal backed off, surveying the scene that he created.

What did it mean?

He needed to remember the exact place and the exact words, of Illusion's death. He loved the tiny creature. He also loved Joshua. Who was the child that inhabited his heart and his home? Where were they headed?

Cal shook his head in fear *and* wonder.

Cal grabbed a shovel from the garage and dug a shallow hole by the tree. It didn't take long. He wanted to remember exactly where he buried Illusion. When Cal was finished, he said a short eulogy.

I'm sorry Illusion. You never had a chance.

Cal thought of her cuddled against him, purring . . . his eyes filled with tears. Was he crying for the kitten or his son? He put the shovel away and paused before entering the house. What was he going to say? What was he going to do? What kind of monster was his son?

His mind battled reality. Aldi was right – Joshua was just a broken kid who needed fixing. Maybe more fixing than most, but he could be fixed. Right? Isn't that what Aldi said? The kid was beautiful on the outside; he *had* to be beautiful on the inside.

Cal escaped to his workshop. He had just received a shipment of greenish-brown Sassafras wood that came from Missouri. Cal laid out the planks and measured them for a new bookshelf, slipped on his safety goggles, and cut the planks. The ear-splitting sound of the saw felt good. He piled up the rough pieces and placed his father's beloved claw hammer with the bright red handle on top. Then he headed for the shower. He turned on water as hot as he could tolerate, and scrubbed with Aldi's green mineral soap, trying to remove all traces of Illusion. When he was finished, Cal dressed in sweats and headed for the den.

Aldi was sitting on the couch staring into the fireplace. There was no fire. Joshua was in the corner playing with his cars. He pressed a button on the police car and a siren rang through the room.

"We need to talk," Cal said loudly. Aldi jumped; Joshua ignored him. "We need to talk," Cal said again. "We can't go on like this."

That caught Joshua's attention.

"I think we should see Kiran. She has a private practice now and . . ."

"No," Aldi said weakly.

Joshua jumped up. He used Sage's voice. "I'm so sorry Daddy. I'm so sorry Mommy. I loved Illusion. I don't know why Mommy kill her."

He hugged Cal's leg.

Cal was horrified. "Stop that," he yelled.

Joshua backed away. Cal took a deep breath. "You need help, Joshua. Mommy and Daddy need help. We're all going to see Kiran. No discussion."

Aldi opened her mouth to say something but Cal stopped her. "This is my decision and no one is going to question it. I don't ever want to clean up a bathroom like that again – or bury another beautiful kitten."

"What do we tell Beth?" Aldi asked softly.

"Tell her," he paused, "that Illusion was hit by a car."

Joshua hid a smile behind his hand. "It's a great lie," he said softly. "Go for it Daddy."

Cal heard but said nothing.

Kiran

1

Kiran surveyed her office.

It should have been a small space for a struggling therapist in a new private practice. Instead, her parents secured a large office condo on the top floor with a beautiful view. It was painted gray-blue with brown leather furniture and an oak desk. In one corner, Kiran had set up a play area with toys, markers, and paper. A few paintings decorated the walls – soothing oil swirls of trees, mountains, and flowers.

"It belonged to a friend who retired," her mother explained. "We got it for a good price."

Kiran knew her parents didn't get the business condo "for a good price." They wanted her to believe that; anything to get her out of DSS and away from *those* people.

"They have the money," Kiran's husband Morgan, advised. "Accept it."

Kiran was happy to leave DSS; it had become increasingly difficult to balance limited time, expanding caseload, and a suffocating bureaucracy. When one case was resolved, ten replaced it. There were so many children, broken families, and pain. She relished helping people but much of her work had become amorphous, blending into a sea of faces and endless entitlements.

Kiran sighed. Her parents were embarrassed by her job in the social work trenches. They remained distant from Morgan, who had two strikes against him – he was black and a NYFD fireman.

"Couldn't you find a doctor or attorney?" Father, The Senator, asked.

Kiran ignored him. Morgan was a much finer man than her twin brother Robert, whose goal was to bed every eligible woman in Manhattan. Father had little say in either of his children's lives – it was the only way they could survive him.

Kiran's flashy new office offered hope, something in short supply at DSS. Kiran would guide people through her interventions. She needed to feel she had an impact – left her mark on a complex world where everyone struggled to find a connect. It was what Father always said.

Find your place and rule.

Father could rule anything and anyone, like pushing carefully aligned dominoes. Kiran didn't have that power.

"Don't hold it against him," Morgan commented. "He was born lucky. Privilege creates entitlements."

Kiran didn't agree. Why would Morgan get it? He accepted that her parents disapproved of their only daughter's biracial marriage. It had been three years and her parents were forced to do what was politically correct. Kiran got the wedding she dreamed of – a large catered affair in a Manhattan hotel. The guest list was filled with prominent names *and* Morgan's colleagues from the firehouse; it was a social event that made *The New York Times*. The firemen set up a grand entrance while Father's buddy, the Fire Commissioner, watched with approval.

Father called it the *bigs* and the *littles*. Kiran smiled at the memory.

She was surprised when Cal requested an appointment. She could never forget Joshua. His files resided at DSS but she kept a copy of his Momma's note to remind her of the little boy who began with nothing. Kiran hadn't heard anything about Joshua since the final adoption. She knew that he had found his forever home, the place where he would resolve his attachment problems and grow into a healthy child. After all, Aldi and Cal were Jewish. Jews always made sure their children were fine. It was in their blood.

The call from Cal said something else.

2

"We need an appointment immediately."

"Of course. It's good to hear from you."

"We'll fill you in when we see you; just make sure we have enough time. I'll pay for as much time as necessary – whatever it takes."

"No problem."

"We need to come in as soon as possible."

"Will you bring Joshua?"

"Yes. First I want to speak with you alone. Joshua doesn't need to hear what I have to say."

"I have a lovely waiting room. It's very secure – we can lock the outside door. Joshua will be safe by himself and we can check on him from the camera in my office."

"I'm not worried about Joshua. I'm more worried about your waiting room."

Kiran's heart skipped.

They agreed on a time. Now, as Kiran waited for the family, she thought about the foster parents who cared for Joshua before Aldi and Cal adopted him. Denise Fletcher and Sharon Candido were good people. They said the same thing about Joshua.

This kid is different. He doesn't like me. He doesn't want to be held, to eat, and he can't suck well. He never responds. He doesn't coo or smile. The kid fights everything.

Joshua is broken.

Kiran asked the question that was as old as Joshua. *Did I make a mistake?*

Kiran rubbed her forehead and smoothed her hair. If she had made a mistake, she was about to confront it. What would Morgan say?

End the fire then figure out the cause.

The door buzzer sounded and Kiran glanced at the camera. It was the three of them – Aldi, Cal, and Joshua. She could see that Aldi and Cal were nervous.

Kiran greeted them in the waiting room.

Aldi smiled and shook her hand. "It's good to see you."

Cal nodded. "Thank you for your time."

Joshua wouldn't meet her eyes.

Something was very wrong. Cal had gained weight, his face worn and distraught; Aldi was gaunt, fear etched in her eyes. Joshua fidgeted.

"How are you doing, Joshua?" Kiran held her hand up for a high five. He backed away.

He still can't be touched.

Kiran dropped her hand. "It's good to see you. Here's what's going to happen. Mommy and Daddy are coming into my office to talk. You can stay here and play with the toys. There are lots of things – even markers and paper if you want to color. After a few minutes I'll come out and bring you into the office with us. The outer door is locked so no one will come inside. You're perfectly safe. There's a camera," Kiran pointed to the ceiling, "where you can wave to us. Is that okay?"

Joshua stared at the camera.

"Answer her," Cal snarled.

"OK."

Kiran smiled at Aldi and Cal. "Are you OK with that?"

"Don't mess with anything," Cal warned Joshua as the three adults entered the inner office.

Kiran closed the door and sat in her high-backed, black leather chair. She glanced at the monitor. Joshua wasn't moving, frozen to the spot where they left him.

Aldi and Cal sat on the couch not touching. Aldi was stiff with arms folded tightly around herself; Cal perched as far away as possible, looking everywhere but in Aldi's direction. Kiran glanced back at the monitor to see what Joshua was doing. He had moved; sprawled on the floor sifting through the box of markers.

Kiran began. "What brings you here?"

Aldi opened her mouth to speak; instead, she broke into sobs. Cal watched dispassionately. They listened to Aldi for several minutes before Cal cleared his throat.

"It's Joshua," he said heavily.

Kiran looked at Joshua. He was painting his arm with the red marker.

"It wasn't his fault," Aldi wailed. "You want to blame him for everything. He can't help the things he does."

"Can't help the things he does! Are you kidding? We had this kitten," he explained as Aldi wailed louder. "A tiny fur ball of a thing. So cute . . ." His voice cracked. "I named her Illusion. Joshua tortured and killed her."

Kiran couldn't hide her response. She gasped. Cruelty to animals was a classic textbook symptom. A book she read, by Dr. Robert Hare, popped into her mind.

Most parents of children later diagnosed as psychopaths were painfully aware that something was seriously wrong even before the child started school . . . In the early school-age years certain hallmarks emphasize the divergence from normal development [such as] vandalism and fire setting . . . hurting or killing animals.

Kiran took a deep breath. "Anything else?" Glancing at the monitor, she saw Joshua dragging a chair. He paused and stared straight into the camera as if challenging her.

What was he doing?

"There *have* been problems . . ." Aldi admitted.

"What kind of problems?" Cal demanded.

"I never thought you wanted to know . . . would be interested . . ."

"What kind of problems?"

Kiran caught Cal's eye. "What kind of problems, Aldi?"

"Nothing much."

Kiran and Cal waited.

"Bedwetting," Aldi said softly.

"I know about that," Cal mumbled.

"He doesn't play well with other children. Beth says . . ."

"What does Beth know? She sends her girls to private school where they're coddled."

"Sometimes," Aldi ignored him, "Joshua steals food and hides it in his room. When I ask him why, he just shrugs. He doesn't get embarrassed or sorry or anything. He *always* lies. It doesn't bother Joshua when I find him in a lie. He just denies it. Like the cat. He said *I* killed the cat. Can you imagine?"

"We fight about him all the time. Aldi tries to hide his weird behavior. I'm always asking for more normal . . ."

"He's hurt. You don't understand that he's hurt and broken and needs to be fixed. All you care about are your damn books."

"I stay away because if I say anything you jump on me."

Kiran let them argue for a few minutes. She glanced at the monitor. Joshua had carefully placed the chair next to the bookcase beneath the cam. He stood on the chair, and holding the red marker in his teeth, scrambled onto the bookcase. He crawled up shelf-by-shelf until he was at the top – high enough to reach the ceiling. It was a liability risk. What if he fell? Maybe she should stop him? Yet this was a chance to observe him; make a more accurate clinical assessment. She decided to wait and see what he would do next.

"You love that kid more than me."

"You love your books more than both of us."

Joshua balanced himself on the top edge of the bookcase. He shoved his face against the cam. He looked bizarre – his features distorted. Joshua grinned and mouthed two words.

Fuck you.

Then he colored the lens with red marker.

"Fighting," Kiran said breathlessly, "is not going to help the situation."

Aldi and Cal were quiet. Kiran could only see faint movements beyond the red streaks.

"I don't know what to do," Aldi said finally. "I try so hard but nothing seems to work. Cal stays away . . ." Aldi touched his arm. "I don't blame you. I don't understand why – or what we should do. I always felt that if I loved him enough everything would be okay."

"With your permission," Kiran said, trying to interpret Joshua's red-streaked movements, "I'll contact the school and request a complete psychological assessment. I'll speak to school administrators, psychologists, and teachers. Perhaps I'll go there and observe his behavior in the classroom."

"You won't find anything," Cal said, "he's always been fine in school."

"Not true," Aldi said softly.

"Not true?"

"His grades are awful. I only put the good ones on the bulletin board, and those don't happen very often. I don't tell you about the others because I know you'll get mad." She took a deep breath. "Joshua has no friends and the art teacher says he makes strange drawings . . . I never hang *them* up. Animals without heads, bloody people with arms, legs, and heads cut off."

Aldi and Cal stared at each other, locked in combat.

Kiran couldn't wait any longer. "I'm going to get Joshua." Her heart pounded as she opened the door to the waiting room. What was she going to find? What had Joshua done?

Joshua sat quietly in the corner with a coloring book.

"Joshua?"

Joshua looked up. "Is it my turn?" He asked sweetly.

He was so beautiful. It was hard to believe that this was the same distorted child staring at her through red streaks on the camera. A chill ran down her back.

This kid is really good.

"Mommy," Joshua ran past Kiran into the office. He jumped in the space between his parents, leaned over, and hugged Aldi. "Mommy I missed you."

Cal was disgusted. Aldi grinned sheepishly, reveling in Joshua's inexplicable show of affection. Joshua looked past Aldi so no one could see his face but Kiran.

He smiled in triumph.

3

Two weeks later Kiran sat at a small conference table in Dr. Paise's office, Joshua's primary school principal. Dr. Paise was dressed impeccably and sat stiffly at the head of the table. Mrs. Fay, the classroom teacher, wore a white blouse, black pants, and sat opposite Kiran. Dr. Wayson, the school social worker, was at the other end wearing a pale green shirt and a tie printed with smiling cats. Dr. Hannon, the school psychologist, sat in the strategic middle.

"Behaviorally," Mrs. Fay was saying, "Joshua hasn't done anything *that* bad. At least I can't catch him. He stays by himself – I never see him playing with children. He's in his own world and doesn't care about others."

Paise was silent, a stony look on her face.

"If one of the boys approaches him," Fay continued, "Joshua chases him away or ignores him. The girls don't go near Joshua. They call him silly names when he can't hear. If I ask, the girls say they're scared of him. I've never seen him steal anything but a lot of stuff disappears in my classroom – small toys, special snacks, photos of pets. When I ask Joshua if he's involved he denies everything."

"Denies everything?" Kiran asked.

"Yes. It's always someone else. Joshua lies all the time. If I ask him for homework Joshua says the cat ripped it apart. I know it's not true, but . . ."

Fay paused. A tense silence filled the room and glances were traded, saying more than words.

No one knew what to do.

Kiran thought about the bathroom scene. Of course he's lying.

"Do you question him if you know it's a lie?" Wayson asked, unable to tolerate the silence.

"I don't know why," Fay said slowly, "this has never happened to me before. I'm . . . somewhat afraid of Joshua."

"Afraid?"

"His eyes." She looked down as the color faded from her cheeks. "They're blank – flat – you know what I mean? Like there's nothing behind them."

"Thank you for sharing that," Hannon said quickly. "It tells us a lot about Joshua."

"I'm sorry if I said too much," Fay mumbled. "Joshua does very poorly in school." She cleared her throat and continued in a more professional, objective voice. "He fails most of his tests and doesn't seem to care. When I'm teaching he doesn't concentrate – he fidgets, plays with pencils, and makes odd noises."

"ADHD," Wayson shook his head.

"Attention Deficit Hyperactive Disorder," Fay echoed him. "Yes, that's very true. Maybe medication will work but it feels like something more."

"What?" Paise frowned, showing Kiran that she was in control. "We don't make psychological diagnoses here until children are properly evaluated. Isn't that correct, Dr. Hannon?"

"Yes," Hannon said stiffly. "Today's meeting is about gathering information, not psychological name-calling."

Paise frowned. She didn't like to be scolded.

Fay shrugged. "I'm just the classroom teacher."

"We suspect," Wayson said, rustling the papers in front of him, "that Joshua is ADHD with perhaps a touch of ODD – oppositional defiant disorder."

"Anything else?" Kiran asked.

"I'm not a psychologist," Fay apologized. "I only see what's in my classroom."

"What else?" Kiran persisted.

Fay took a deep breath. "He pushes everyone away. Sometimes he rocks and hums songs to himself, although I know he's not autistic. It's strange. A kid like that usually gets picked on – the boys love to taunt vulnerable ones. Not Joshua. They stay away. It's more than being afraid of getting hit or bullied. Joshua is different – do you know what I mean – he's happy in his own space and they're happy to be away from him."

Wayson chose his words carefully. "I'm not surprised. I've contacted his mother numerous times to set up an appointment but she refuses to come in. The father is out of the picture. Joshua is an only child, adopted, with very little parental support."

"That's not true," Kiran interjected but no one listened. She couldn't take her eyes off the smiling cats on his tie.

"They probably don't discipline him," Paise suggested. "Or socialize him. That might account for his need to isolate."

"Let's not condemn the parents," Hannon interjected, "before we have the facts."

"Joshua is a troubled child," the school social worker agreed. He paused. "I went through his file and there were drawings."

"Drawings?"

"Drawings. Many . . . people . . . felt it was important to keep them in his file. They're frightening." He gulped. "Drawings of animals with their heads cut off and red crayon blood everywhere. Drawings of people with no eyes, holding hatchets or knives, decapitated heads, aliens, and devils." He shook his head. "They're not your Mommy-and-Daddy-in-a-pretty-house-with-a-dog type stuff." He pushed a paper to the middle of the table. "Here's one."

"I asked his mother about the pictures," he continued. "She didn't seem surprised. 'We had a lot of road kill on our street' she said."

There was a tense silence.

"Whenever I talk to him, Joshua won't make eye contact, doesn't respond, or is verbally inappropriate."

"Verbally inappropriate?" Kiran asked.

Wayson cleared his throat. "He asks . . . questions."

"What kind of questions?"

The social worker grimaced. "About my sexuality." He spoke so softly that it was difficult to hear.

Paise shifted her position. "That *is* inappropriate," she muttered, relieved not to discuss Joshua's artwork.

Kiran looked at him quizzically. "Can you give me an example?"

Wayson lowered his eyes. "One day I saw him in the lunchroom. Joshua smiled. Then . . . he asked," Wayson paused. "He asked . . . do you . . ." Wayson struggled with the words.

"Do you . . . fuck . . . boys or girls?"

Paise caught her breath. Fay turned her head away.

Wayson's face turned deep red.

"I'm sure that was very disturbing," Kiran tried to soothe him.

"How did you respond?" Hannon cut in.

"It was awful," Wayson whined. "In these times . . ."

Kiran completed his sentence. "It could be devastating."

Wayson nodded, pleased that she understood his dilemma.

"So," Kiran added sympathetically, "you stay away from him just like the children?"

"Of course . . . unless necessary."

"Well," Paise took over, "it's clear that Joshua needs help and although we offered it to the parents, they've resisted. I'm glad they consulted with a private therapist."

Kiran winced. Politically correct and psychologically mute solved a lot of problems. "What about Joshua's learning problems?"

Wayson attempted to conceal his relief. He pulled at a non-existent beard and tried to look Freudian.

Hannon shook her head. It was always the same dance. She spoke evenly, with confidence. "I'm in the process of preparing a full psychological report. My preliminary findings indicate that there is a large scatter with significant delays in speech and language. His IQ falls in the normal range so with help, he should be able be able to improve his language skills. However, I believe we're seeing a picture of ED – emotionally disturbed – that can develop further as he enters puberty."

Kiran sighed.

You think?

"We may be seeing early signs of severe mental illness," Wayson supported the psychologist. "I hate to say that about any child . . ."

Paise glared at him. Schools were masters of euphemism.

"If the parents allow us," Wayson returned to a safer subject, "we can provide group support for socialization skills."

Group support? How do you get a Reactive Attachment Disorder kid to work in a group?

Kiran said nothing.

"I assume," Paise added, "you'll continue to see Joshua and his parents in private treatment?"

Kiran nodded. "Let's keep in touch. I'd like updates from you on any changes – any problems."

"Of course," Paise agreed. "Doctors Wayson and Hannon will be in regular contact with you."

Kiran doubted that anyone would call her unless Joshua did something like set fire to the building or kill the cats on Wayson's tie. They were too afraid of litigation.

"Thank you," Kiran said formally. "If I can be of any help, don't hesitate."

I didn't see this coming six years ago, Kiran thought.

What don't I see coming six years from now?

Paise stood up from the conference table and the others followed. "If you will excuse me, I have another meeting . . ."

Wayson fled the room, Fay and Hannon lingered.

"I don't know where this child is going," Hannon said softly, "but it's not good."

Kiran met her eyes. "His parents are good people but this is beyond them."

Hannon shook her head. "Eight years old," she sighed. "Only eight years old."

"It's like a book," Fay added. "Once the words are printed and bound you can't change them. I'm sorry for him. He's such a beautiful boy – it's like there's nothing inside."

Nothing.

And perhaps there never will be.

4

When testing was completed and the files stored permanently in the school record, Kiran met Aldi, Cal, and Joshua in her office.

"What did the school say?" Aldi asked.

Cal played with his fingers. He gets it, Kiran thought, even without the facts.

"They had a lot to say," Kiran began. "Joshua, I asked Mommy and Daddy to bring you here because I think you should know everything. We shouldn't keep secrets."

Joshua didn't respond. He meandered over to the play corner.

"Joshua," Aldi said sharply, "listen."

Joshua ignored her.

"It's OK," Kiran said. "He hears us – he's listening to everything we say."

Joshua's shoulders stiffened.

"There are several problems. All of them can be handled," she lied. "There are learning disabilities in reading and language . . ."

Aldi clapped her hands. "That's it! Of course – I should have known all along."

Kiran shook her head. "There's more," she said but Aldi was already making plans.

"We can get help," Aldi said breathlessly, "do home drills, projects, help Joshua read better."

"Let her talk! Kiran – continue."

"There are emotional and psychological issues that need to be addressed." Joshua's back was to her but his sudden lack of movement gave him away.

"No problem," Aldi said happily. "We'll deal with the learning disabilities and he'll be just fine."

"No," Kiran said sharply, "we need to deal with more than learning disabilities."

A strange image filled Kiran's mind. There was a carpet of dying leaves with one, scarred, blood-red leaf in the middle, as if taunting the others. Was Joshua that leaf?

"Aldi," she said sharply. "You need to be realistic."

Aldi shut her down. "I *know* my child."

Kiran turned to Cal. "I want you to listen to what the school said. Listen carefully."

Cal nodded as Aldi ignored Kiran's summation of the discussion at school.

"What's a learning disability?" Joshua asked in his sweetest voice. He grabbed a toy truck and came back to where they were talking. Kiran resisted the urge to duck.

"When you learn in a different way," Kiran said. "You need help catching up to the other kids."

"What other kids?"

Joshua was baiting her. His voice was sweet, his stance was innocent, but his eyes were flat and removed – blue pools gathering ammunition.

"Kids your age. You use different ways to learn, which means you need extra help."

Joshua nodded solemnly.

"You see, dear, you're just like the other children. You just need a boost of sorts," Aldi smiled happily.

Joshua did an eerie dance. He looked at his mother and grinned sweetly. He looked at his father and frowned. Then he turned so they couldn't see his face, shook his hips and looked at Kiran. He mouthed one word.

Fuckers.

Kiran was taken aback by the family theater. Joshua caught her. He narrowed his eyes and tensed his body as if ready to pounce. It lasted only a few seconds before he turned to Aldi.

"I want to be like the other kids, Mommy," he pleaded. "I really want to be just like them. I want you and Daddy to be proud of me. I don't want any of those learning things."

He forced out a few tears and made his voice shake like a television commercial for *Save the Children*.

"Yes," Aldi cried, "of course we'll make everything right. We're proud of you with or without learning disabilities." She opened her arms and Joshua fell into a reluctant hug; Cal patted him on the back.

Cal's voice was shaky. "Of course we love you and are proud of you."

Kiran watched, knowing the scene had been artfully orchestrated by Joshua. He turned to her with his back to his parents and flashed a grin that sent shivers down her spine.

Was she lying to Aldi and Cal? Was there hope? Joshua returned to the play corner. He sat on the floor and hummed a song to himself. Kiran took a deep breath. She couldn't work *without* hope. She had to do something so she outlined a treatment plan.

"The school will set up extra help for reading and language. The special education teachers will report to Wayson and Hannon, who will write an IEP – Individual Education Plan. If there's any . . ." Kiran paused, thinking of the cat. "Emergencies at home or in school, call me as soon as they happen." She looked at Aldi. "No waiting – as soon as they happen."

Aldi nodded; Cal's eyes clouded. Joshua headed to the play corner.

"Cal, your job is to spend more time with Joshua. Go places with him – do things that you both like. Perhaps you can bring him to the store. Joshua might find it interesting."

Textbook treatment plan. To what end?

"Joshua," Kiran said firmly. Joshua stopped but didn't turn around. "Joshua," she repeated, "turn around." Slowly Joshua faced her.

His blue eyes were ice.

"Look at me," she commanded.

He struggled and briefly met her eyes. "Life can get much better for you," Kiran said, not believing her words. "All you have to do is work with everyone; they're all on your side."

Joshua studied his fingers.

"Aldi," Kiran switched her focus. "Your job is to be more consistent. Don't let Joshua get away with things."

How can Mommy stop him from killing cats?

"Be more vigilant; don't be afraid to say 'no.' "

Aldi nodded. "He doesn't listen."

"I know. Make sure there are consequences when he doesn't listen and rewards when he does."

"Of course."

The kid doesn't care about that either.

"Do you have any questions?"

Aldi and Cal shook their heads.

Joshua grinned at Kiran. "One question," he said sweetly. "Who really killed the cat?"

5

Kiran stared at her empty office.

There are some things I can't fix. But I have to try.

What had she done when she worked at the DSS? She was so anxious to make things work; give history and home to an abandoned infant. She recalled what Morgan had said.

We always do our best but sometimes there are fires you can't put out; homes you can't save. It's all part of the job.

Was Joshua one of those fires? Did she really do her best at DSS?

Kiran bowed her head. It slipped in like an unwanted friend sneaking through the back door. Denial. Sigmund Freud believed that denial was one of the best defense mechanisms. People don't face reality; instead they reject the facts in spite of overwhelming evidence. Denial was a cover-up for unwanted truth.

Sometimes it worked and sometimes it was very dangerous. In a chilling twist, denial was necessary for good parenting. Would a parent tell a child who's not very smart that he's dumb and will never amount to anything – even if it's the truth? Parents *have* to believe that their children are smarter, prettier, and more skilled to build self-esteem and instill confidence. Similarly, telling a child that he's a genius when he failed all his tests or is a gifted musician when he's tone deaf hurts everyone. Where does denial end and truth begin?

Especially with Jewish parents. Everyone *knew* that Jews want their kids to be doctors and lawyers, not plumbers and electricians. Little Joshua had been placed in the perfect home to assure healing and success. Right? Kiran still couldn't avoid the question.

Am I in denial like everyone else?

She took a deep breath. Suddenly she saw Joshua as an old, molding red leaf surrounded by the dead. Kiran shuddered. It was just her imagination. Joshua would get better . . . things would change. It had to – right?

The words returned unwanted.

There are some things I can't fix. But I have to try.

Her hands trembled.

I have to try.

The red leaf clung to her like an image that couldn't be erased.

Joshua

Thank you. Thank you. Thank you.

1

Everyone watches me. I get smart. There are lots of cats out there. Sometimes I stare at the squirrels and birds and dogs. What is it like to stick pushpins in them? Flush them down the toilet? I want to do it but Mommy and Daddy watch me all the time so I have to be good.

What does it mean to be good?

Mommy brings me a set of superhero dolls with ugly faces and rubber swords. I kill them. I steal her favorite knife – the one she uses to cut steak and chop vegetables. She calls it *Forged Premio.* I cut off the superhero heads and I leave for Mommy.

She screams. It's the coolest scream, better than a horror movie. She takes the bodies and heads and puts them in a black plastic trash bag. She hides them in the garbage. When Daddy comes home and asks what happens to my superhero dolls, I smile.

"We gave them away," Mommy says.

Auntie Beth comes with her two bitches, Danielle and Sage. I act nice. When no one looks, I steal their baby dolls and bring them into my room. I take the knife and dig out their eyes.

My finger is cut. I watch me bleed. It doesn't hurt. I taste blood and think of vampire movies. I look at the dolls and put cuts on their necks. I rub my finger so the eye holes have real blood. I stick the dolls in the bitch's backpacks. It's fun watching them play until everything stops and they open their backpacks and they scream. Mommy doesn't know what to do.

"Joshua," she cries, "did you hurt the dolls?"

I use my sweetest voice. "I would never do that."

The bitches scream louder.

"Then who did it?" Auntie Beth asks.

Only Auntie Beth sees my smile.

Mommy looks at my finger. "Joshua tell us the truth."

"It *is* the truth," I grin and point to the bitches. "They did it."

The bitches scream louder and Auntie Beth doesn't believe me.

"Go to your room," Mommy points a finger at the stairs.

"Sure," I laugh. "Anything you want."

I do the stairs. Mommy talks to Auntie Beth, "please don't tell anyone about this. Not a word to Cal. He won't understand that boys will be boys."

I hide at the top of the stairs.

"How can you keep this kind of behavior a secret?" Auntie Beth says. The girls stop crying and Mommy gives them each a chocolate chip cookie. My cookies.

The bitches are eating my cookies.

Now that pisses me off.

"He's *broken*," Auntie Beth says.

"Broken?" Mommy sqeals. "How can you say he's broken?"

"He is. Can't you see that? Joshua is broken."

Mommy's voice is scary. "Don't say that about my son."

"It's true."

"I think it's time for you to leave."

"Aldi . . ."

"I hope you have a nice drive home," Mommy says.

I hide in my room and Auntie Beth and the girls get their stuff. There's a knock on my door. It's Sage.

Sage is two years older than me. She has big hazel eyes and red hair. We stare at each other.

"I don't hate you," she says.

I laugh.

"I know you're sorry."

"Not."

Sage shakes her head. "You're not all bad. I know it." She digs into her pocket and offers a chunk of chocolate. "Try it."

I laugh and make a mean face. "You think chocolate fixes everything."

"I know."

"How do you know?"

Sage eats the chocolate. "Chocolate makes everything better."

"Asshole."

Her eyes get big. "You don't scare me."

"I had fun cutting your doll. You should try it."

Sage's eyes fill with tears. "No one can be that bad."

"Try me."

We look at each other.

I squeeze my finger until it seeps drops of blood and run it across her chest, leaving bloodstains on her pink shirt.

"Sage," Auntie Beth calls, "where are you? We're leaving."

Sage reaches across the space between us and pushes me hard. I stumble but don't fall.

No one pushes me.

"I know that you're not all bad," Sage cries. "I just know it." She turns and runs downstairs.

That day I learn it's a lot more fun smashing people than toys.

Except for Sage.

2

Two weeks later Auntie Beth is back.

Sage whispers, "let's talk."

We meet on the concrete step in front of the house. We sit. I stay far away. Sage knows not to touch me. Mommy makes sure *everyone* knows not to touch me.

"I want to be friends," Sage says.

"After I kill your doll?"

Sage nods. "After you killed my doll."

"Why?"

"I know that you're not all bad. I just know it, so I decided I want to be friends."

Something shifts inside.

"Best friends, forever? BFF."

"You're not scared of me?"

"I'm not scared of you."

"OK," I say. "You can be my BFF."

3

Now I have to be good and I have a BFF and I have to figure it out. How?

When people talk they smile. I don't like to smile. I watch other kids. They smile at Mrs. Fay and they smile at each other. They laugh. It's hard to be like them. I don't get it. I think about moving my mouth to look like a smile.

I practice on Mrs. Fay. At first she gives a weird look but I keep on doing it and the weird goes away.

"You look happier Joshua," she says.

What's happy?

I smile hard. She believes me.

"You have a beautiful smile Joshua. Do you know that? You're a very handsome boy."

I smile more. I test the kids.

It's not easy to smile at kids. They don't like it as much as Mrs. Fay – they make funny faces and run away. What does that mean? I see boys carry balls; soccer balls, baseballs, and basketballs; all that stupid stuff. I smile and carry a ball. I like soccer balls the best. When I dribble, I'm kicking a kid or dog who screams. That makes me feel good. I look around. No one knows what I think. No one knows that my soccer ball is on fire and will burn anyone that comes near it.

Awesome. I own the fire.

I carry my soccer ball and smile. One day kids ask me to play. I don't know how but they don't care. I smile and smash the ball. I kick it further and higher than the other boys.

That makes them smile at me.

I practice with Dr. Wayson. He calls me into his office a few times a week. "How are you feeling, Joshua?"

Like I want to kill you.

I smile.

"Are you playing with the other kids?"

I smile and tell him about kicking soccer balls.

Assholes.

"It's good for you to play sports," Wayson says, making a note on the paper in front of him. "It makes you more popular."

Fuck the cats on your tie.

I smile and Dr. Wayson is happy.

Then I learn something – thank you. If I smile and say thank you, I fool everyone. I say thank you and think fuck you. Cool.

"Thank you Dr. Wayson," I smile.

Fuck you.

"Wonderful," Dr. Wayson says. "You're really doing well."

"Thank you," and I smile bigger.

Fuck you.

Thank you, Mrs. Fay. Thank you Dr. Paise. Thank you Dr. Wayson. Thank you Dr. Hannon. Thank you kids for letting me play soccer. Thank you. Thank you. Thank you.

Fuck you. Fuck you. Fuck you.

I control everyone. Mommy is so happy with her good boy that she stops crying about Illusion. Daddy looks at me different. They buy me stuff I don't like. Soccer shoes, baseball hat, baseball glove, bat. Stupid stuff. I know what to do.

Thank you. Thank you. Thank you.

Fuck you. Fuck you. Fuck you.

I'm king. I control them. I tell them what to do. All of them.

All the fucking kike assholes.

That's when Daddy brings the laptop home. "Try it," he says.

Daddy shows me how to go on the internet and get sports scores. Big deal. Then he shows me You Tube.

"You can watch kids play soccer and have fun."

Fun? What's that?

4

Daddy leaves me alone with the laptop and I look for cool stuff and find Tyler Hadley. He lives on You Tube. He kill his parents with a hammer and celebrates by throwing a party for forty Face Book friends. No one at the party knows about the dead bodies he left in the bedroom. Tyler is my new BFF.

No one knows about me either. I leave my new laptop on the table in the turret playroom. It's my best toy – another BFF.

After a few months people don't care. No one watches me on the computer. No one watches when I pat a teammate on the back after he makes a goal and I hit him really hard. No one watches when I hug my cousin and hold on until she can't breathe.

Auntie Beth *sees*. It's in her eyes.

"Hi Auntie Beth," I smile. "Thank you for coming. Thank you. Thank you. Thank you."

Her eyes squint and she frowns. She goes into the kitchen and talks to Mommy.

"He's all better now," Mommy says. "Now that we have him in therapy with Kiran and the school is working to address his learning disabilities, Joshua is a new child. It's amazing."

Auntie Beth sniffs. It's a sucking sound. Swallowing snot.

"No really," Mommy says, "see for yourself."

Auntie Beth looks over Mommy's shoulder and sees me listening. She doesn't say anything. She just looks. I say the words without sound. It's a warning.

Fucking kike bitch.

Leave me alone.

Auntie Beth's face twists into an awful smile. "You're not fooling me," she says softly.

"What?" Mommy says. "I couldn't hear you."

Auntie Beth sighs. "It's wonderful," she says to Mommy, "I'm so happy he's changed."

Mommy gurgles with pleasure.

I wonder if there's any You Tubes on how to kill an aunt? Squash her? Fire her?

The only one I like is Sage. My first BFF.

Sage sits with me on the front step while Mommy and Auntie Beth drink weird tea called *Tibetan Tiger*. Sometimes Grandma Espie joins them. Grandma Espie and Sage have the same red hair and creepy hazel eyes. Grandma watches me all the time. She doesn't say anything. She just watches and plays with that dumb thing on her neck.

Sage and I stare at the big bushes next to the step – they look like hairy monsters. What would it be like to impale someone on the peak of the roof then push them down over the edge into the bushes?

Sage pulls out some *Endangered Species* chocolate. She hands me a square.

Sage and her fucking chocolate.

"Grandma Espie and I trade chocolate," Sage explains. "One day we found this dark chocolate with deep forest mint. It's one hundred percent ethically traded. The cocoa comes from small family-owned properties and helps sustain habitats and communities."

"Big shit." I toss the chocolate on the grass. No bite. No clue what Sage says.

Sage looks at the chocolate in the dirt. She takes a bite out of her own square and eats it slowly.

"I'm not scared of you, Joshua," Sage says. "You can't change my mind."

I don't look at her. "You should be."

"No I shouldn't. I'm not like the other kids."

"Fuck off."

"No."

I turn to make a scary face and yell hard. Something stops me. Her eyes. I never look into people's eyes but Sage grabs me and pulls me in.

"Leave me alone," I say but don't mean it.

Sage is quiet. Her eyes do all the work. They take hold. I float in water – a warm cocoon inside a dark belly. Voices soft and distant like music in the shadows. Music and nightmares.

A voice snakes in; hard and ugly.

I hate you. I hate you.

Die.

My heart races. It's going to burst from my chest and disappear into red shadows. My body trembles. There's a power that wants to leave me lifeless. Sage touches my hand.

"Joshua," she whispers, "BFF."

The voice crawls into my body and shocks every cell. I'm alone. I'm always alone.

The voice calls herself Joshua's Momma and leaves me with strangers, rips me from her. Please come back. Please don't leave me. I need you. We're supposed to be one. Don't you know that?

Where do the questions-without-answers come from?

"You're not alone, Joshua," Sage says.

A scream rises. Slithers my insides until it bursts out like a snake – Illusion's death howl. Sage backs away. I run from Sage, the Gothic peaks, the chocolate in the grass.

"Do you want more chocolate?" Sage cries. "It will make you feel better."

Nothing makes me feel. Better.

I run through streets of old houses and new houses and dead trees. I run into the park. I run until I'm sweaty and sticky and I see only anger anger anger. I can't run anymore. My breath hurts. I sit under trees. On the flat rock.

That's when I see the stray dog. Dog. *Dog will die. For Sage.*

When I get home I search You Tube for ideas.

5

Someone else sneaks into my life.

"This is your Great Aunt Hanya." Mommy says. "She's Grandma Espie's sister. You have known her all your life."

Big shit.

"Hello," I say sweetly.

The bitch has curly brown hair and mean eyes.

"She's a psychologist," Mommy adds. "I told her how you ran away and she said she wanted to meet you."

"Why?"

Mommy and Great Aunt Hanya frown.

"She's your Great Aunt. Grandma Espie's sister," Mommy says again.

"So?"

"She lives in the city – in a cool apartment. Would you like to visit her?"

"No."

Great Aunt Hanya tilts her head and tries to see inside me. "I have a big TV in my apartment and a terrace outside. Would you like to hear about it?"

What the fuck is a terrace?

"No."

Great Aunt Hanya shakes her head.

"Why did you run away, dear?"

Mommy and I laugh at the same time.

Dear?

Great Aunt Hanya reaches into her big tote. "I brought you something." She pulls out a lime green monster truck with big black rubber wheels.

"Thank you. Thank you. Thank you."

I grab the monster truck from her hands and run up the stairs into the turret playroom. I hear Mommy talk.

"I'm sorry he's so rude."

"That's ok. Just keep him in therapy. He needs it."

"It's learning disabilities. Don't you see that?"

"It's more than learning disabilities. Open your eyes."

"Thanks for coming," Mommy says stiffly as she leads Great Aunt Hanya to the door.

"Espie asked me . . ."

"Of course. Joshua is just fine. You and my mother don't have to worry."

The door opens and closes.

"Joshua," Mommy calls from the bottom of the stairs. "Do you want some cookies?"

I have a cool answer.

I throw lime green monster truck down the step. It bounces and breaks apart. A zillion pieces. A wheel hits Mommy on the leg. She rubs her leg and picks up the pieces.

Thank you. Thank you. Thank you.

Dog

1

Kiran smiled at Aldi and Cal. They were in her office for a couple's session. "I'm getting very good reports from school," Kiran said. "Joshua is polite. Sometimes he plays with the other children, although he still tends to isolate. I'm told he's good at soccer."

Aldi grinned; Cal looked doubtful.

"Language extra help," Kiran continued, "helped him improve in the classroom. Mrs. Fay reported that his grades are better although he still fails many tests. She said he's trying now – something he didn't do before – and he smiles a lot so she thinks he's happier."

"I knew it!" Aldi clapped her hands. "It was all about learning disabilities. All that psychological stuff . . ."

Kiran stopped her. "Joshua's improved but he's still Joshua. You have to be realistic. He has a lot of problems and . . ."

"No," Aldi shook her head. "Now he hugs me."

"Does he hug you, Cal?"

"No."

"Nobody gets better *that* fast," Kiran said softly. "You need to be vigilant."

Aldi had to believe that Joshua was normal. Everything would be fine once he caught up.

Was that also Kiran's truth? She thought about Joshua's last session.

Joshua had come in to her office while Aldi sat in the waiting room. The day was dark and gloomy, a raw chill in the air entered along with him.

Joshua settled on the couch.

"Things are going well?"

He refused to speak.

She sighed. Kiran hated therapy sessions with long, tense silences. "I have good reports from the school."

Joshua's blue eyes were like slabs of ice. No feeling. No expression. Kiran shrugged off a foreboding that was worse than the gray day outside. Joshua curled into a corner of the couch while Kiran ran her fingers through her hair, rubbed the back of her neck, and played with the pen in her lap. She waited for him to speak.

Suddenly he stood up. "It's too bright in here." He turned off the overhead light. The office was bathed in shadows.

"You don't like light?"

Joshua gave her a strange look. He circled the office. "I like it dark. Dark feels better." He laughed, an odd, ingenuous sound. He went to the play therapy corner and fiddled with some of the toys. He picked up a small green truck and flung it against the wall. It shattered.

"Why did you do that?"

Joshua shrugged.

"Do you like to break things?"

Joshua examined the broken parts of the truck as Kiran watched. After several minutes, he piled up the pieces. He returned to the couch, sat down and stared absently at the ceiling.

"Do you like to break things?"

He tilted his head and smiled. It was a brilliantly rehearsed smile, full of artificial sun and cheer.

"That's a nice smile."

It collapsed.

"Fucking bitch."

"Me?"

"Fucking bitch."

Kiran didn't respond.

"It's OK if I say fucking bitch because you said I was safe. I can say anything I want and you have to listen because Mommy and Daddy pay you."

"I did say that you're safe here."

"Fuckingbitch. Cocksucker. Motherfucker. Assholekike." He rattled off the words like multiplication tables.

Kiran assumed a poker face.

"Good shrink. Goodyshrink. Goodygoodyshrink."

"Is that the way you feel?"

The smile returned. "Thank you. Thank you. Thank you." As if he was performing lines for a school play.

Kiran shrugged.

"Nothing freaks you. Nothing at all."

"No."

"I bet I can blow you away if I want."

Kiran shook her head. "I've seen a lot of things – a lot of troubled kids. I bet you can't."

"Can."

"Can't."

"What would you say if I told you I had a razor blade in my mouth?"

"I wouldn't believe you."

"What would you say if I told you that every time I've been here, I've had a razor blade in my mouth?"

"I still wouldn't believe you."

Joshua grinned. "You're not very smart, GoodyGoodyShrink."

"Smart enough."

Joshua shrugged.

He opened his mouth and stuck out his tongue.

There was a single razor blade on his tongue. Kiran stared, stunned. There were only two words to describe the scene.

Joshua wins.

2

Kiran forced herself back to the present. What should she tell Aldi and Cal? What could they do with a child like Joshua?

Does anyone know?

"Learning disabilities," Aldi said in a singsong voice. "That's all it ever was. Now they're taking care of the problem. My Joshua is going to be just fine."

Kiran caught her breath. "No Aldi, it's a lot more than learning disabilities. I told you that from the beginning and I'm repeating it now. Joshua is very troubled."

Cal leaned forward. "What are you saying?"

"I'm saying that Joshua needs more than extra help in school. There's a part of him that's very hurt."

"Broken," Cal mumbled.

Aldi glared at him.

"Broken," Kiran echoed, "and it's going to take a lot to fix him – if he's fixable."

"How can you say that?" Aldi cried. "He has learning disabilities. Are you going to give up on him because he has learning disabilities?"

"I'm not giving up on him. You need to understand what we're dealing with."

Aldi stood up. "I won't tolerate this. I'm not going to listen. Joshua is fine – he's a little boy with learning disabilities. That's all."

"Aldi . . ."

"No!" Aldi screamed. "That's all you and the school want. You need to make Joshua into a . . . demon boy. I won't let you – or anyone – do that. I have to protect my child." Aldi's eyes were wild. "I have to protect my child," she repeated. "If I don't, no one will."

"*No demon boy,*" she hissed, making odd, sucking movements with her lips. "Do you hear me?"

She opened the door and ran out of the office.

Kiran went after Aldi but it was too late. She was gone.

"See what I have to deal with," Cal scowled when Kiran returned. "She refuses to see what's right in front of her eyes."

Kiran backed up and closed the waiting room door. Her heart was pounding. She didn't want Cal to see how much Aldi had disturbed her. She slowly returned to her chair.

Take a deep breath.

"Are you telling the truth?" Cal asked quietly.

"The truth?"

"The truth about Joshua."

Kiran chose her words carefully. "My work isn't a science," she explained. "It's an art. You can't predict an outcome the same way you predict numbers or chemical reactions. It doesn't work that way."

"Then only tell me what you think – how you *feel*."

She hesitated.

"Do it," his voice was steel.

Kiran took a deep breath. "Joshua does have learning disabilities."

"And?"

"He's troubled. Very troubled. His behavior implies serious psychological issues that go beyond learning disabilities."

"What?"

"Diagnoses are intellectual name-calling. We need to deal with behaviors rather than names; people rather than indictments."

"What is it?" Cal demanded. "I want a diagnosis not psychobabble."

"It's better to think . . ."

"I want a diagnosis!"

"If I have to call it something," Kiran closed her and took a deep breath. "It's conduct disorder."

For now.

"What's conduct disorder?"

She was on familiar ground. It was easier to be clinical. "A conduct disorder is a group of behavioral and emotional problems in children and adolescents. Kids with conduct disorder have problems following rules and behaving in socially acceptable ways. A lot of adults and children see them as 'bad' rather than mentally ill. Conduct disordered children have negative attitudes – they fear and don't trust others. It's hard to reach them. They tend to be aggressive toward people and animals, destroy property, lie, steal, refuse to pay attention to the rules and consistently violate the rights of others."

Cal's shoulders sagged. "What's the prognosis?"

Kiran felt cornered. "They need a lot of treatment. Adolescents are high risk for anti-social behavior, substance abuse, chronic conflicts, aggression, sexual precocity . . . many people see conduct disorder as the most difficult illness to treat in childhood . . ."

"And when they grow up?"

Psychopath.

She couldn't say the word. Aldi and Cal were good people. How could Kiran pass such a hopeless sentence on their son? She forced her most clinical voice. "Symptoms tend to persist – aggression, conflicts, alcohol and substance abuse, anti-social behaviors, criminality . . ."

Cal listened intently. "It's that serious?"

"Yes."

There was a tense silence.

"Is there anything I can do?"

"Support Aldi. Even if everything is OK now, something will give and . . ."

"I understand. It's like the cat – something will always happen."

"I hope not, but . . . yes. Something will always happen."

Cal's eyes filled with tears. "Anything else?"

"Spend time with Joshua. Give him a strong male figure to emulate. Show that you love him – share your life."

Cal covered his eyes. His hands trembled as he processed her words. Kiran waited, giving space to his grief.

"We never should have adopted him. I knew it but Aldi wanted . . . " He shook his head angrily. "It's a little too late for that."

Kiran wanted to cry with him. She once had such hope for Baby Joshua Doe.

"Thank you," he muttered. "Thank you for the truth. They don't dare say these things in school."

"No they don't. Most parents react like Aldi. They don't want to hear it so they blame the school."

"Will you stay with us – with Joshua? Will you help us?"

"Of course. Maybe I'm wrong . . ."

Cal stopped her. "I'm not going to fool myself. That's Aldi's job."

She looked at him with empathy. "I'll stay with you, Aldi, and Joshua. I'll do whatever I can to help."

Cal nodded. "Thank you."

A single tear trickled down his face.

3

So the fucker wants to spend time with me. Something Kiran says. Maybe the razor blades? She never tells Mommy and Daddy about *that*. It's what she calls *confidentiality*. I call it stupid but that's why I'm smarter than all of them.

Daddy isn't a pushover like Mommy. I have to be more careful. He likes the smiles and thank you's and hugs but the kike doesn't always buy it. He looks in my eyes for answers. I hate that. I don't like anyone to look in my eyes. Except Sage.

It goes on for a long time – until my tenth birthday. Ten is a good number. Doing Illusion in the bathroom is dumb. I know how to smile and say thank you and pretend I'm an asshole now so everyone believes me except for Auntie Beth. I can act like anyone – fool anyone – except her. Those fucking eyes. I want to gouge out those fucking eyes but it's stupid and I'm not stupid.

I log on to You Tube and look for more BFFs. Like Alex and Derek King. I watch them in court, on the news, in family pictures. The brothers are twelve and thirteen years old and they kill their father with a baseball bat and set fire to the house.

I want to be like Alex and Derek, so I tell the girls in my class that I'm going to kill them. If they tell the teacher, Mrs. Zane, I'll kill their best friends too.

Mrs. Zane buys it. She thinks I'm the perfect kid. She's doesn't look into my eyes – she sees my smile and hears my thank you's.

I want to kill Mrs. Zane. Maybe slit her throat and watch the blood bubble out.

I read that if you cut across the neck from the jugular and through the carotid arteries it only takes five seconds to bleed out. I count off five seconds on my fingers. Cool.

Once she bleeds out I can cut off her tits. Chop off some fingers. Stab her all over. I dream about it but it's stupid to do anything and I'm not stupid.

I do their game.

I play with boys and aim soccer ball at them, not the goal. Most get out of the way. What a rush. Screams when my kick gets a head or gut or dick. I send one to the hospital. They say it's a concussion.

Concussion.

Now that's a cool fucking word. After that they don't ask me to play. It's funny. If they only knew the truth about my plan. Fire at Walden Pond. Mommy and Daddy love that park. Walden Pond. What a stupid name.

Sage gets it. Or doesn't get it. I'm not sure. Most people see around me. Never *in* me. Auntie Beth gets me but never sees inside me. Sage jumps in and wanders. She touches stuff I don't know is there. Then she smiles and whines.

"You're not all bad, Joshua. You just want everyone to think that."

I don't *care* what everyone thinks. Except Sage. I wonder what Sage will say about Dog. She knows about Illusion but never says her name not like Auntie Beth who wears Illusion all over her face or Danielle who's scared of me. It would be fun to stick them with pushpins.

Sage is different. Even though Dog is her fault I won't tell her my plan.

I see it first on You Tube. They set a dog on fire and he howls and runs and flames. The video goes viral. I want to go viral, too. When Sage makes me run away and I find Dog in the park I think about the video. Dog is brown with curly fur and a dirty tongue. His paws are muddy and he smells. It keeps people away. They think he's sick. Dog isn't sick but people are really stupid. He weighs about forty pounds and has dark, dumb eyes and a big tongue. After I see the You Tube video, I make my plan. First I bring Dog food. He doesn't come close. I bring strips of steak I steal from dinner. They're red and bloody, the way Daddy likes it. Mommy calls it *rare*. Black-and-blue. Dog can't stay away. The dumb fucker trusts me. Dogs are stupid but so are people.

We make friends and I tell him his name is Dog.

Then the dreams start.

Dog in the middle of the fireplace in flames. Daddy tells me that's what they do to kikes who don't like church. He calls it the Inquisition. Instead of a shooting or hanging, they tie people to wood stakes and burn them.

Cool.

Daddy calls it a funny name. Auto da fey.

Burn the kikes.

What does it feel like to burn alive in fire?

I watch Dog and think about it. I study the video. Then I make a plan.

Dog lives near trees that look like wood stakes. He sleeps on dead grass, leaves, and twigs that make a great dog bed between the trees. A dog cave! That's how I figure it out. It's fun to burn a dog cave with Dog inside. I steal lighter fluid, long matches, and fatwood from the fireplace. Daddy never misses them. I put steak inside the house for Dog – *rare* pieces because Dog loves them the best. Dog comes right to me. He trusts me. I pet him on the head and he wags his dirty tail.

Dumb fucker.

I toss the steak onto his bed in the tree cave and he goes after it. Dog can't stop and he eats everything.

He'll die happy.

I push rocks and branches against the cave. Trap him. There's a look in his eyes. I don't know dogs can scare – I guess it's like a cat.

Anything can scare except me.

I squirt the lighter fluid on Dog's back. He whimpers. I throw in some fatwood.

Dog watches. He doesn't know he's trapped. I take matches, light them, and toss the fire into Dog's cave to see what happens.

It's better than Daddy's flames in the fireplace. The fire leaps up really high. Dog cries but there's nowhere to go. He barks and howls and cries and jumps and scratches and throws his body against the trees, rocks, and flames. Like the video in real life.

The flames snake inside me. I'm powerful – more powerful than a superhero.

The flames go high, the park is on fire. I want to hold the fire, eat the fire, become one with the fire. I hear the sirens. The firemen are coming.

That knocks me back into smart.

I smile at the fire and hide. I watch the whole movie and no one knows.

The firemen come and the police come and a lot of people and kids come. I slip into the group behind the police. Everyone is quiet, hypnotized by the flames. The firemen put it out quickly and I'm sad they kill the fire so fast. A black fireman turns and looks at the crowd of people. Our eyes meet.

It's weird. Fucking weird.

He knows.

I hide behind kids until he can't see me. Dog is toast, fire is out and everyone leaves. I hate to look into people's eyes but this guy traps me. I have to get away from the eyes.

We talk about fire at dinner. Mommy and Daddy use a new word.

Arson.

4

I never heard *arson* before. I turn it over and over in my mouth until it tastes really good. Arson. It's a beautiful word.

I dream a lot about arson but Mommy and Daddy never know. They think I'm a little boy excited by firemen and police.

"Horrible," Mommy says.

"Who would want to set a stray dog on fire?" Daddy asks.

"A homeless guy?"

"Teenagers?"

"At least Walden Pond is safe," Mommy says.

"The fields and the rest of the park are safe," Daddy adds.

"It was a small fire, thank God."

Small fire?

Fuck you.

They look at me and Illusion is in their faces.

I make a sad face and inside I laugh. Yeah Dog is cool. But it's worth it for the fire.

"Poor Dog," I say. "Who would do that?"

Mommy and Daddy are satisfied.

The next day Sage and I sit on the front step. She asks me a lot of questions. Like she knows. It doesn't take long to convince her

I'm innocent. She holds something she calls *fair trade* chocolate – *Green & Black's*.

"Fair trade," Sage says, "means people aren't exploited to grow or make the chocolate. There are no slaves in *this* chocolate."

I like the idea of slaves. "Don't you wish you had a slave?"

Sage ignores me. "It comes from Belize."

Where the fuck is Belize?

Sage unwraps a red-and brown bar called *Maya Gold*. It's got orange and spices.

"Taste it." She gives me a chunk of chocolate.

Maya Gold tastes like outside this world. Outside of me. I don't like it. Maybe Dog would like it? I laugh inside.

Sage giggles. "It's really different." She eats a chocolate rectangle. "Did you hear about the dog in the park?"

"Yeah. Cool." I grin. I can't hide much from Sage.

"Cool?"

"All the firemen and stuff. Boys love that."

"Cool?" Her voice is hard. "How can you even *think* that setting fire to a dog is cool?"

"Dog," I correct her. "His name is Dog."

She's silent. "You knew the dog?"

That's when I realize Sage is not quite like me.

I know what to do.

"Everyone knows Dog. Don't you?"

"No."

I shrug.

"This isn't funny." She fumbles for more chocolate.

"No it's not funny."

Sage's eyes fill with tears. She takes another rectangle of *Maya Gold*.

I think Sage is different but only a *little* different. She doesn't like fire but she likes me.

"See," I rub my eyes, "I'm crying for Dog, too."

Sage stares at me. She has more questions but is afraid to ask. Suddenly, my dick gets hard. What the fuck is *that* about – I'm not even a teenager? I cover my crotch with my hands.

"See," I say again. "I'm crying for Dog, too."

Fucking Sage.

She believes me.

The Senator

1

It wasn't easy but Cal took Kiran's advice to include Joshua in his life. Aldi knew it was difficult.

"Let him in to *Tree of Life,*" Kiran advised.

Cal was skeptical. "I don't want to risk my business." .

"He's your son," Aldi insisted. "There's no reason why Joshua would hurt anything."

Cal frowned and Aldi knew he was reluctant. In the end, Cal loved his son and wanted to do anything that might help. He took the chance.

"I want my boy to carry on our name," Cal confided, "to be there when we get old."

Aldi doubted that Joshua would ever become the boy Cal wanted. Joshua was cold and distant, his eyes flat and unresponsive, his smile no deeper than the curl of his lips. Cal complied because there had to be hope. He brought Joshua to *Tree of Life.*

In the beginning they waited for Joshua to fail; but as the months passed he learned to dust and shelve books, straighten stacks on the tables, and carefully unpack cartons. Cal taught Joshua about first editions, values, and salesmanship. He shared stories about authors, publishers and antiquarian finds. Joshua soaked in everything, remembering names, books, titles and dates.

"Thank you Daddy. Thank you. Thank you. Thank you."

"This might work," Cal admitted to Aldi.

She hugged him. "Of course it's going to work – Joshua's your son."

"It's strange," Cal continued, "he greets people, thanks them, and smiles a lot. The kid is actually *charming.*"

"See," Aldi grinned, "Kiran was wrong."

One day in front of Aldi, Cal said to Joshua, "I'm proud of you, son. Can I shake your hand?"

Joshua held out his hand.

They shook hands in a manly ritual. The grip was a bit tight, Cal thought, probably because Joshua was showing off his strength.

2

Aldi never thought it would happen. Things changed. She knew that time can be the author of illusion but chose to be convinced that Joshua was a normal, regular kid.

One Sunday morning Aldi stayed in bed while Cal and Joshua left for the store. The wind howled like feral cats as Aldi lingered, thinking about how their lives had improved. The worst was over – no more dead cats, gouged doll eyes, or decapitated super heroes. Beth visited and Danielle stayed close to her while Sage forged a friendship with Joshua, happily sharing her chocolate. Family holidays were peaceful – the kids and the adults didn't fight – and Joshua was respectfully quiet.

Was life approaching normal?

A vision of The Senator drifted into her mind. Aldi smiled. Perhaps for the first time in his life, The Senator had been wrong. Joshua wasn't a demon boy.

Aldi still kept her secrets. She would never tell Cal or Kiran *everything*. She refused to talk about the dead insects fried with a magnifying glass or birds with broken wings left on the grass. She avoided mentioning a dissected squirrel behind the bushes. The bedwetting continued; Aldi washed the sheets and acted like it didn't happen. Joshua didn't hug them but he said the right words even if his eyes were blank.

"The eyes are windows to the soul," Beth observed. "I don't see his soul."

Aldi was horrified. "How can you talk like that?"

Beth shrugged.

Aldi had tried to pierce the glassy surfaces that were Joshua's eyes. "I want to look into your eyes."

Joshua made an odd, primal growl and ran away. She decided not to pursue him or the subject. It was easier to pretend it didn't exist.

The school presented more problems, talking in letters rather than words.

"He's ED not just LD," Dr. Wayson said warily. "With a touch of ADD, of course. I'm afraid for his future."

Dr. Paise agreed.

"He's Joshua," Dr. Hannon said. "We need to work with the child not the letters."

"No," Aldi argued. "It's straight LD – I've read the research. The social problems go along with the diagnosis."

Paise and Wayson shook their heads, Hannon sighed, and everyone clung to their opinion. As long as Joshua wasn't disruptive or dangerous, it didn't matter.

Aldi sighed, slipping out of bed to begin her day – a few hours behind Cal and Joshua. She packed a brown bag with lunch and headed for *Tree of Life*. She didn't notice the dark car parked at the curb; her eyes were fixed on the entrance. She walked into the store and went straight to the register.

Aldi loved the store almost as much as Cal. She savored the smell of old books, carved leather covers, and worn suede bindings, delighting in the discovery of voices from different centuries. She enjoyed the customers – bibliophiles who relished being around old books; readers who wanted to hold the originals; and historians seeking solace. Many spoke unhappily of a shaky future where reading would be done only on a screen.

Joshua watched as she entered the store.

"Hi Joshua. I brought you and Daddy some sandwiches and cookies."

His face was blank. "Thank you Mommy."

Cal was standing behind a stack of books. "You'll be very happy with your selection," he said to a customer.

"I always am."

Aldi froze.

The voice. I will never forget it.

3

Cal saw Aldi before she could escape.

"Aldi, I would like you to say hello to The Senator," Cal said obsequiously as he and his customer approached the register. "You worked with him in the Teach Washington How! campaign."

She didn't need to be reminded. Aldi felt sick; her heart pounded and her stomach did odd, nauseating flips as if she was riding an out-of-control roller coaster. She clung to the lunch bag and her hand cramped.

The Senator smiled like a man who controlled everyone.

Aldi didn't know what to do. She hadn't seen him since the day he had given Cal the book, *Murder at Pizza Baas.* Aldi had begged The Senator for secrecy about their affair, afraid she might lose Joshua. The Senator traded sex for silence.

Aldi stared at his face, terrified at what he might do or say. He gazed at her, his eyes lifeless. Although he was seventy years old, The Senator looked the way she remembered him – a powerful, compelling man who fucked awestruck young women. He still had the flat, glazed charisma that could beguile anyone who didn't know better.

"It's good to see you," she said slowly, her tongue thick.

He shook her hand. Tight, firm grip.

"And this is my son Joshua," Cal said. "This is our United States Senator, son. He's a very important man."

The Senator held out his hand to Joshua. Joshua refused the gesture; his eyes narrowed and his lips twisted into a frown.

Demon boy. The Senator's words reverberated in Aldi's head. That's what he called her son.

"I never liked shaking hands either," The Senator said. "I have no choice. Occupational hazard."

Joshua was silent.

The Senator turned to Cal. "It's wonderful to meet your family."

"The Senator comes here often," Cal said proudly.

Often?

Often? Why didn't she know?

"Well," The Senator smiled ingeniously. "As often as I can. I'm in Washington most of the time."

Aldi wanted to scream. She wanted to hit him, gouge out his flat eyes and medicine-man smile.

See what you did to me? To us?

She couldn't move.

"This time," The Senator continued, "I brought you something. I don't think it has any material value but it's fun to own – a vintage article from the White House."

Aldi doubted every word. *He's a liar*, she wanted to yell at Cal. *A liar*. He probably had twenty thousand "vintage articles" to distribute. The Senator gingerly presented a tiny blue box and Cal grinned stupidly. He pried open the box and there was a small brass engraved cigarette lighter with 'USA White House' and a line drawing, complete with American flag, on the front. On the back, in the same engraved letters, were the words, 'A gift to my very special friend' and The Senator's unmistakable signature.

It probably cost him ten cents. Purchased in bulk.

Cal caught his breath.

"It doesn't have great value because people don't smoke much anymore, eh Cal? At least they don't let anyone see them smoke. Politically correct, you know what I mean? Actually, this lighter is almost an antique. I think the proper term is *vintage*. I thought you might enjoy it."

The Senator spoke as if giving a political speech. "It still works," he added, taking the padded box from Cal, lifting the lighter and snapping a flame.

The flame reflected in Cal's eyes. Aldi was wrenched between the flame, Cal, Joshua, and The Senator.

How can Cal be so stupid?

Aldi looked at Joshua. Perhaps he was smarter and didn't buy The Senator's campaign? Perhaps he could see more than most people in the state?

Joshua was mesmerized by the flame. He licked his lips. Aldi watched her son and a chill ran through her – more unnerving than The Senator standing so close to them. She read Joshua's lips.

Thank you. Thank you. Thank you.

4

I see him in my dreams.

The Senator.

Daddy is happy with The Senator and His gift. Daddy smiles. Daddy is happy that The Senator goes to his store and buys stupid books.

Stupid boring books. Stupid boring Daddy. Stupid boring Senator.

There is something about The Senator. He's all face, nothing else. He talks and smiles and he doesn't mean it. Mommy acts weird like the day she finds me with Illusion. Her face changes when she sees The Senator.

My face never changes. I never feel. What is it like to feel? Mommy feels so *much*. Maybe because she's a mommy or a woman or something like that? I'm not sure. Whatever she feels, it's a lot.

Now it's about The Senator. Weird. The Fucking Senator. What's so great about him?

He gives Daddy a stupid cigarette lighter and Daddy acts like The Senator hands him a million dollars. I like a million dollars. I can buy a lot of stuff with a million dollars. What good is a piece of shit lighter? Daddy promises to keep it on his private desk in his boring stupid office where he can see it all the time. If Daddy does that no one will see but Daddy and me. The Senator wants everyone to see his name next to the White House. Is The Senator the next President? He's kind of old but who knows? Presidents can be kikes too.

I don't get grown-ups. They're supposed to see everything but they see nothing. They never see me, only what they want. They don't see The Senator either. I think he gets it. That's why he gives strange looks and lighters with his name on the back. Does he like to kill animals? Kick kids? Set fires? Does he wet his bed and hate to be touched? Does he dream of darkness and devils and superheroes with their heads cut off?

That night Daddy brings home a new book called *The Great Fire* by a guy named Jim Murphy. Jim Murphy loves fire like The Senator. Daddy and I read it together. We sit on the couch in front of the fireplace and read about the 1871 Chicago Fire. Cool. Daddy reads and I look at the pictures. Daddy brings home more books – *Famous Fires* and *The Firefighter's Best Friend: Lives and Legends of Chicago's Firehouse Dogs*. I tell him that I love firemen, fire engines, and fire dogs.

Mommy watches and smiles. She forgets about The Senator and talks about the holidays. She's going to make *latkes* and *sufganiot*, Hanukah donuts, and light the menorah. Candle fire.

5

A few weeks after The Senator's visit, the store gets busy. Daddy smiles. People start buying lots of books. It's boring. Daddy goes from customer to customer. Sometimes Mommy comes to help. Everyone forgets me. I wander; no one cares. I eat all the candy in the dish by the register and no one cares. I dust shelves and stack books and no one cares.

I'm fucking bored.

I go to the back of the store. A customer looks through old books on cows, farming, and weather. Who cares?

I see the back exit.

I leave and cross the space between the store and Daddy's tiny office building. It's an old, ugly shed. I don't know why Daddy loves it so much.

I shake the door and I'm in his office alone. I look on the shelves. Big shit. I go to Roycrofter's Corner and look at stupid kike shit. There's an old ashtray. Cigars? Cigarettes? Fire? I think of the Chicago Fire and Dog and *Lusitania*.

A movie comes to life.

I close my eyes and watch it in my head. People eat. Rich people. Laugh. Chew bread and cookies and sandwiches. Eat fancy chocolate like Sage. I see the German U-boat – a devil snaking to the cruise ship.

Lusitania. The Unsinkable Ship.

I think of the book Daddy shows me called *Lusitania: An Illustrated Biography of the Ship of Splendor* by some guy named Layton. Doesn't Daddy think about anything but books and bookshelves? Four tall smokestacks are on the *Lusitania* when it heads for Liverpool and boasts that no one can get her. No one can get her. No one can get me. The story bursts into flames. Dog. Chicago. Fire rumbles in her hold. The ship sails by the lighthouse and a kid sees it all. Lucky kid.

The movie gets brighter, the sounds louder, bands play, people party, and the German U-Boat spits out two torpedoes, one after the other, that speed through the water and rip into the side of the great Lusitania. *Daddy tells me everything.* Panic and fear and 1200 people die. The ship is a rusty heap of junk in a water grave. And fire.

Fire that eats everything and kills everything.

I can make fire, too.

I sit in Daddy's chair and pretend I have all the fire in the world. I look at the stuff on the desk – the books, papers, postcards, and sticky notes. I roll down the desktop and then I see it.

The Senator's lighter.

I take the box and open the top. It grins at me. The brass lighter with 'USA White House' and picture engraved on top. The Senator's signature on the back. I see The Senator's face – his fake smile and blue eyes. Daddy thinks he's the greatest man in the world.

I can make fire, too. In Daddy's office.

I pile up books, papers, sticky notes. I take The Senator's lighter and click on the flame and touch it to the paper and wait.

How can paper burn that fast? The old books are in flames before I realize what's happening. The fire travels, hot yellow fingers snake across the desk. It goes beyond the desk and licks a book shelf. The books burn. The flames move faster until fire covers the wall. I want to stay here forever with the fire. There's a voice inside, clear and strong.

It knocks me back into smart.

Get out.

I crawl out the back door between the flames. People are screaming and pointing; no one sees me. I hide behind a garbage can and grin. The sounds roar – fire trucks, alarms, hungry flames, Daddy's screams.

Joshua. Joshua. Where are you?

I slip from behind the garbage pail and run into his arms.

"I'm OK Daddy. I'm in the store when it starts."

I'm OK fucker.

Daddy holds me so tight I want to kill him. I peek around his trembling body. I watch firemen race to the building with hoses and axes. I listen to them call above the hiss of the fire.

Then I see him.

The black fireman.

The one I see in the park when Dog burns and the trees burns and . . . he pauses and our eyes meet.

I hide behind Daddy and the black fireman goes to work.

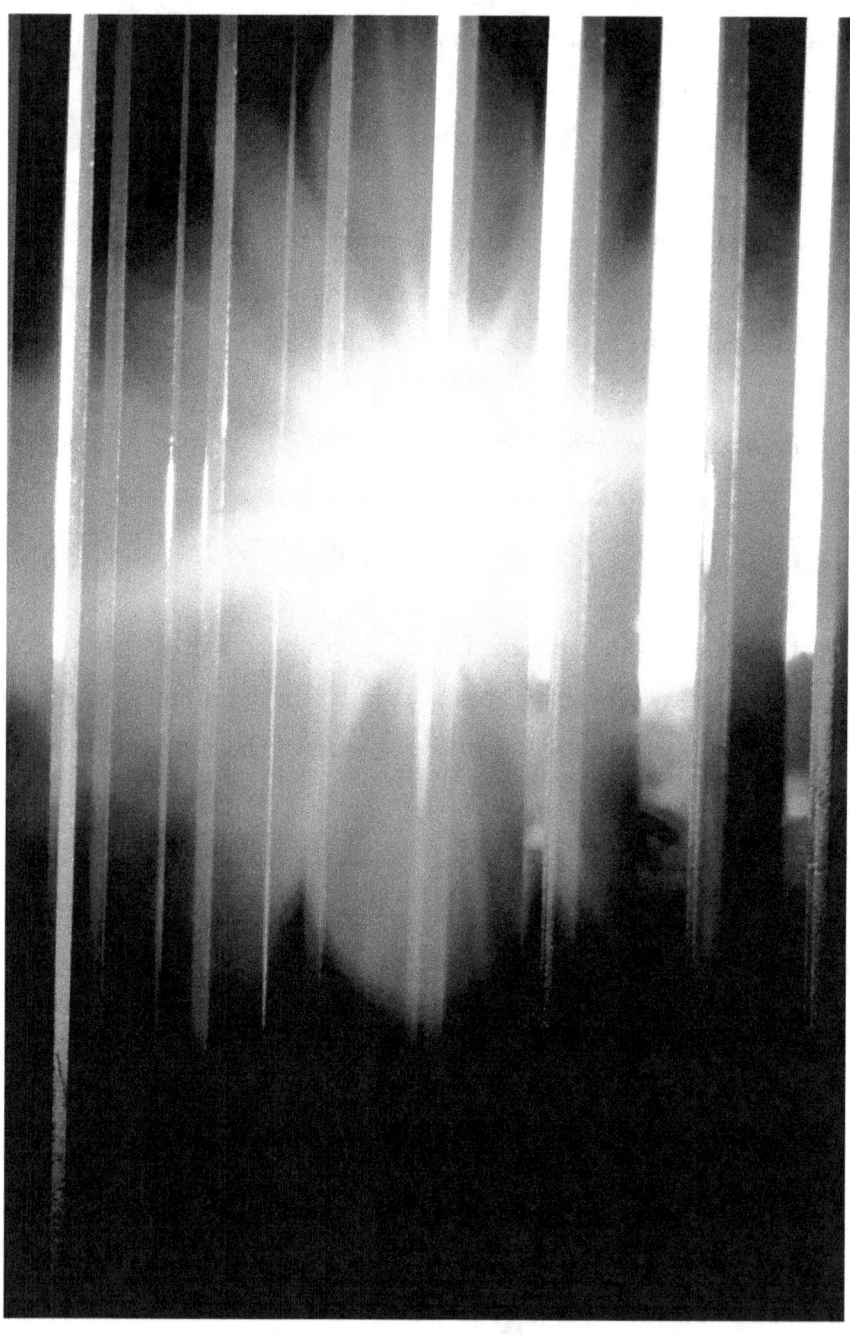

Sage

1

Grandma Espie laughed. It was a sweet sound.

Grandma and I sat in the kitchen with a pile of exotic chocolate, playing the trading game. It was just the two of us, no one else was interested in our connect. Mom and Danielle were shopping, accustomed to leaving us alone during chocolate time.

"You know Sage and Grandma," Mom explained to Danielle. "They love to hang out. I think it's the red hair, hazel eyes, and that strange dark complexion."

She was right. Grandma was my favorite – even more than Joshua. I loved to sit, listen to her stories, trade chocolate, and imagine what life was like when she was my age. Once Grandma told me about her mother and *their* chocolate game.

"Mother and I played the same way," Grandma explained. "It's a gift from the past."

The game always started with the same question, "which do you like better, Grandma? Today I have *Bovetti* with cocoa beans and *Theo* organic fair trade cherry and almond."

"How about *Scharffen Berger* nibby?" Grandma grinned.

"I would rather have *Madécasse* sea salt & nibs any day."

We dissolved into laughter, a shared moment between generations. Grandma softly thanked 'Mother, God, or whatever force in the cosmos that brought us together'. I heard every word. I loved the sound of Grandma's strange prayer and the connection to a past over half a century ago. It was the same feeling with the chocolate – another link to our odd legacy, along with red hair and hazel eyes. Chocolate was a power beyond candy.

Sometimes, Grandma would frown and talk about family legends. My favorite was Esperanza, the fifteenth century girl who bludgeoned a Portuguese soldier to death so he wouldn't rape or kill any more Jewish girls.

Maybe it was her name that touched me?

"They're in your blood," Grandma would tell me. "Don't ever forget their courage – strong, proud women determined to protect our people."

"Aren't we lucky now?" I would try to soothe her. "We're safe in New York."

"Never." An edge always crept into Grandma's voice. "We're never safe."

Then she would say the words I hated.

It doesn't matter who you become, what you do, where you go. As long as any part of you is Jewish, no one forgets. They will *find you.*

Why wouldn't Grandma believe the world had changed?

"Try this," I would give Grandma a piece of *The Tea Room* Midnight Mocha.

Grandma would smile indulgently and return to our game.

"Interesting," Grandma said thoughtfully. "High cacao."

"Seventy-two percent. It beats *Nestle's* Crunch."

That was our private joke: *Nestle's Crunch, Hershey's Kisses,* and *Kit Kats* were chocolate for the uninformed. We were the chocolate elite.

One day, Grandma's eyes turned very dark and serious. Her smiled faded and I knew that she had something important to say. "I want to talk to you about Joshua."

I shrugged. I hated talking about Joshua.

"He's done some very bad things."

"The dolls? Illusion?"

"Yes. And more."

"He's not all bad, Grandma."

"No, Joshua is not all bad but he's broken. He's done terrible things. Do you know what that means?"

"I guess."

"You need to do more than guess. I know you love him but you have to be smart. Sometimes boys do crazy things that we don't see coming. He needs help – the kind you can't give him."

I frowned. "Joshua would never hurt me."

"I don't know . . ."

"He's all talk – he just likes to scare people."

Grandma touched her hamsa. "I know you care but people aren't always exactly who you want or believe them to be."

"Aunt Aldi believes in him. So does Uncle Cal."

"Joshua is their son. They have to believe in him."

Grandma was thoughtful; her words harder to say than eating cheap milk chocolate. Grandma was worried. I remembered the day Joshua and I sat on the front step talking and suddenly he screamed and ran away. I never knew why he was so afraid. I didn't tell Grandma about *that*. It was my secret.

"I won't give up on Joshua," I said instead. "I can't. He's my BFF."

"BFF?"

"Best Friend Forever."

"Forever," Grandma echoed softly. She shook her head. "Don't give up on your BFF – just be careful."

I broke off another piece of *Bovetti* dark chocolate with cranberries. "It's so good. Here." I held out my offering.

Grandma took the chocolate but didn't smile.

"I know you're trying to warn me," I said, "but you're wrong on this one."

"Read this," Grandma gave me a few books. "We can talk about it or not – whatever you want. Just read and think of Joshua. Promise me."

I nodded.

"Now," Grandma said, "back to chocolate. Do we have any *La Maison du Chocolat*?"

2

I couldn't refuse Grandma, although I knew she was wrong. She just didn't understand Joshua – like everyone else. After our game was over and Grandma went home, I thought about her request. Mom and Danielle were putting away their new clothes so I opened the book written by William March, called *The Bad Seed*. It was the story of Rhoda Penmark.

She just went on eating her apple, shaking her head, and looking us over with that calculating, almost contemptuous look . . . the other pupils both feared and detested her.

Rhoda Penmark was a child murderer. Why did Grandma want me to read the book? Joshua wasn't Rhoda Penmark – yet the description was haunting; I *saw* that look in Joshua's eyes, how the kids reacted to him . . .

I checked out *The Bad Seed* online. The book had been a hit, selling over one million copies and winning the National Book Award. It was made into a long-running Broadway play and a movie that won an Academy Award. Rhoda's character was based on a real-life serial killer, Belle Gunness, who killed twenty-five to forty people around the turn of the 20th century.

No one knew the exact number.

The story affected many people. The phrase "bad seed" became synonymous with evil child. I knew that people loved to read about cold-blooded young killers. Did it mean there were a lot of bad seeds, Belles and Rhodas, living among us?

Were the bad seeds Grandma's *they*? Where did Joshua fit in?

I read some of the other stuff Grandma gave me – stories about Joshua Jenkins, Kip Kinkel, Larry Swarz, and Columbine's Trench Coat Mafia, Dylan Klebold and Eric Harris. The list of young school shooters and mass murderers was long and growing. Books with names like *Kids Who Kill* and *Killer Kids* were terrifying. Is that what Grandma thought of Joshua?

If the kids weren't caught, they grew up to be serial killers like Jeffrey Dahmer, Joel Rifkin, and The Iceman or non-murdering psychopaths like Robert Moses and Bernie Madoff.

Grandma hated Robert Moses.

I wondered if the killers were like the men Chana and Esperanza murdered. Or were they like Chana and Experanza themselves? Was Grandma warning me that someday she would murder someone? Had she already murdered?

I thought of sweet, gentle Grandma and couldn't imagine her in the bloody mess of murder. I decided not to worry. If Grandma held secrets, I didn't want to know. As for me? My hair was red and I had hazel eyes but my name wasn't Chana or Esperanza. I was different.

I shifted my focus back to Joshua. There were a lot of questions.

The next time I saw Grandma, I gave her *NibMor* extreme, *Lindt* dark with a touch of sea salt, and asked, *why?*

"They're all around us," Grandma shivered. "I remember the most famous psychopath in New York history. Aldi and your mother were young teenagers and I was terrified that he would find them. Sam Berkowitz stalked Queens, killing young couples in cars. In all, the Son of Sam murdered six people and wounded several others. He was adopted as a baby by good Jewish parents."

"And you think Joshua is like *him*?"

"I don't think anything, Sage. I just want you to be aware. Many of these men were adopted; broken at a very young age. My mother used to warn me that people like this were evil. No conscience. No empathy. No remorse. No compassion. No feeling."

"How can you say that about Joshua, Grandma? He has lots of feelings."

"Does he?" Grandma asked as she sampled single origin *República Del Cacao* from Ecuador.

It was bitter.

3

A few days later, Grandma Espie showed up with Great Aunt Hanya.

Great Aunt Hanya was the patriarch of the family. As a Doctor of Psychology, her word was always taken as truth. She was consulted only on big problems, like when Joshua killed the cat and Aunt Aldi tried to keep it secret.

I looked at Great Aunt Hanya's unflinching eyes and smiled weakly. Grandma couldn't kill but was Hanya capable of great evil?

"I can't stay long," Great Aunt Hanya grabbed me in her gaze. "It's a very busy day."

She was always busy.

Hanya pointed to the couch in the den and indicated that I should sit. Grandma stood behind me where I couldn't see her face. Hanya settled in a chair opposite me.

"We need to talk." Great Aunt Hanya began.

I nodded. I was terrified of what she might say.

"Your grandmother is worried," Hanya continued. She rested her hands in her lap.

"About what?"

"You needn't be afraid of me."

"I'm not."

"Are you sure?"

I nodded.

"Good. You must know that I always bring the truth. I don't lie."

"I know."

"Good. Now back to your grandmother's concerns."

"Yes."

"Joshua."

I forced a smile. "Joshua is fine."

"No, Sage, Joshua is not fine."

"Grandma worries too much."

"Grandma is *right*," Great Aunt Hanya said in a steely voice. "Joshua is not to be trusted."

"He would never hurt me."

"He would never hurt anyone unless he got the chance."

"I don't understand."

"I know you don't understand, but I do. Too well. Joshua has already done some terrible things. Do you know what I mean? He can't change. He won't change. Joshua will only get worse."

"All those things he did were mistakes. He's very sorry."

Great Aunt Hanya leaned so close that our faces were almost touching. Her voice cut like a sharp, well-honed knife. "Joshua is never sorry. Don't forget that. He can't feel – he can only pretend."

For a moment, I saw the look in Joshua's eyes when I spoke to him alone after he gored our dolls.

I had fun cutting your doll, Joshua snarled. You should try it.

Hanya glanced at Grandma. "I have to confess. I often wondered about the dog and Cal's office."

"The dog in the park?" I spoke softly – not wanting to think about Uncle Cal's office. Everyone had said it was an electrical fire . . . called it arson.

"Someone set those fires."

"You think it was Joshua?"

Great Aunt Hanya shrugged.

"I know Joshua didn't kill Dog."

"Dog? The animal had a name?"

"Yes."

"How do you know?"

"Joshua told me. Everyone knew Dog, but Joshua was very sad about him."

"What makes you say that?"

"I saw him crying for Dog."

"When?"

"On the front step. Joshua told me he liked fireman and stuff. You know, all boys like that. Dog getting killed made him sad."

Grandma Espie and Great Aunt Hanya exchanged a strange look. I turned around to look at Grandma.

"What's going on?"

Grandma shook her head.

I stood up and backed away. "You're both wrong. Joshua is good – why can't anyone see that? How can you think he set those fires?"

They didn't respond.

Was I the only one who understood Joshua?

I remembered what Joshua said when I asked him if he had heard about Dog. He took it back but now it made me wonder – the word sent shivers down my back.

Cool.

Six Years Later

Psychological Summary Update

Student: Joshua

School: Memorial High School

Age: 15 years 11 months 2 weeks

Joshua's ego functioning is problematic, with distortions in reality that can potentially lead to paranoid ideation - viewing the environment as a threat. His gap between receptive and expressive language leads to frustration and anti-social behavior. He lies easily and convincingly, uses simple phrases to express anger and smiles inappropriately. He demonstrates conflict in artwork with sadistic themes. Joshua has the potential to act out his violent fantasies.

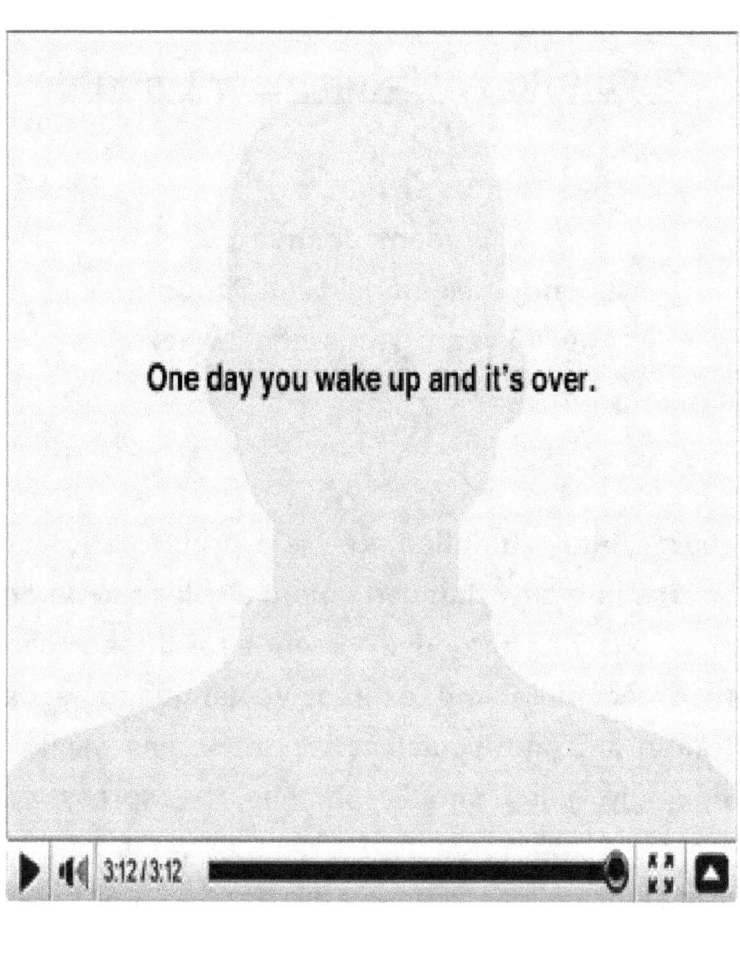

Monday

1

I'm the only one *alive* in this mess of brown, dead leaves.

I stare at my artwork. It's black and gray in greasy sketch pencil. In the middle, *center stage,* is a thick tree with twisted branches spread across the page. On each branch is a rope with a noose and a dead man. Maggots wiggle in eyes, ears, nose, and lips. Death smiles, skeletons dance, and shiny white bone laugh in grinning skulls. In the corner is a snarling biker. He wears a black leather robe, a bird-head, eyes that spit fire, and a Nazi Iron Eagle.

"That's very . . . interesting, Joshua." Mr. Bailey, my art teacher, shudders and looks over my shoulder. His skin is pale, his lips curl. Bailey is an old bastard with a puffy face, wrinkles, and thin strands of hair stained brown and gray. My art teacher says he's a sculptor outside the classroom. The fucker can't make anything but noise. Lots of pig noise like grunts and snorts.

"It's my dream," I say. "The one I have last night."

Bailey nods. His jowls tremble like the dead men on the gallows. "You like it?" He asks. "You like the . . . subject . . . of your drawing?" He gulps, his Adam's apple bobs like a fish lure.

Of course I like it, asshole. That's why I drew it.

"It's very dark," Bailey adds, swallowing hard. His breath hisses in his throat.

What's it like to slit throat and spurt blood? Slice Adam's apple like a ripe red delicious? Silence the fucker's voice? Cut deeper and watch everything drip over his shirt? Over my drawing? How long does it take to die when you start with an Adam's apple?

"Interesting," Mr. Bailey says.

I jam my hand into my pocket. I have deep pockets; I wear jeans over black, steel-toed Dr. Martens with shiny silver eyelets. My white sleeveless tee shirt is a skull and crossbones. The school hates the way I dress. They send notes to Mommy who ignores them.

"You can dress any way you want," Mommy says. She tears up the notes.

Good Mommy.

No one knows I have a tattoo of a Nazi Iron Eagle with lightning bolts on my thigh. I flex my leg and it looks the bolts come from my dick. No one has a dick like me.

I play with the brass cigarette lighter in my secret pocket. On the front is a sketch with the words 'USA White House' and an American flag. On the back is the words, 'A gift to my very special friend' and The Senator's signature. It's a souvenir from my fire that burns Daddy's office. No one knows I have the lighter or set the fire.

"What are these?" Bailey asks and points to the corpses.

Teachers are so fucking stupid.

"Dead men," I smile.

"Dead men?"

"Yeah. Aren't they cool?"

Bailey's Adam's apple bobs harder. "Why?"

"Why are they dead?"

I know his gig. It's a shrink's question. The kike takes my art and brings it to the psych office to "analyze" my work and figure out what I'm thinking. Why don't they ask me? I tell them. I tell them good.

"They were bad."

"Bad?"

"They broke laws. They die. They broke lots of laws. Do you want to know what they do?"

Bailey nods although it's clear he doesn't want to know.

"Well," I point to the first corpse. "This guy kills teacher. He bashes head with a baseball bat. This guy stabs pizza dive owner. With a big knife. The third guy hammers father's face. And the fourth guy burns school."

Bailey clears his throat. He makes poker face and wants to end the questions but the old bastard is stupid. "And these?" He points to the skeletons.

"Cleaning crew. They wash blood and clean tree for the next takers."

"I see."

"Of course," I use my sugary voice, "it's all a dream. Not real."

"Wouldn't you like to draw different things?" Bailey points to the kid next to me. He draws an ugly beach with fat fucks swimming in the water under a hot sun. No smarts. Colorful, mushy bodies like Play Doh.

"Boring," I say loudly.

The kid turns when he hears my voice. His forehead wrinkles and he goes back to work.

No one fucks with me.

Bailey rubs his chin.

The bell in the hallway rings. We look up. I hate those fucking bells. I feel like Pavlov mutts we learn in science class – ring a bell and drool. Even Dog is better than that.

"Can I keep this?" Bailey asks lightly.

"Sure," I grin and stand up. "Thank you. Thank you. Thank you."
Bailey gives a weird look.

"For liking my art," I add brilliantly. I'm much smarter than assholes. I get them to like anything.

"Yes," Mr. Bailey nods.

I get my books and head for the hall and leave my dream on desk. My notebook covers are the same – bikers, aliens, gallows, skeletons – it freaks everyone. I like that. Bailey rolls up my dream and slips on rubber band. I like the snap of the rubber band – it bites skin. I stop at the door and look in the hall. As soon as kids see me they part, leaving a Red Sea path for me. Great movie. I watch it in class about old movies. Those guys love blood and gore like me. Moses and his kikes.

No one likes me at school – they all stay away. They don't see greatness. I know more about the world and life than all of them. I know the world is messed up and no one can fix it – there are too many gangs, too much violence, too much hate . . . yeah, I know all that.

It would be different if Sage is here. She goes to a private school with a fancy name. Like Danielle. Aunt Beth is only happy with fancy.

The kids and jocks and bullies stay away from me. I'm not a big guy and I'm skinny. My hair is caramel-colored which isn't cool. Maybe someday I'll dye it? Sage says it's hard to know me even though I'm so cool. Sage talks a lot. She's eighteen and thinks about college. She wants to go far away and live on a campus. I tell her that it isn't happy. Sage is the only one who's not afraid. It's cool to have her around.

I know Sage never leaves me. She can't – she needs me too much. Why trade Joshua for fucks who talk about history and science and stuff? No worry. Sage does what I want – I have that power.

Sage and I have history. Pictures fill my head.

We sit on a flat rock in the park close to where I burn Dog. Sage shows me her latest discovery.

"It's called *Chocolate Moderne*," she waves a green and red and black wrapper. "Lime, dark chocolate, toffee. Delicious."

I grunt. I don't get Sage and her chocolate. Most of it tastes like crap but I *like* to watch her eat it. Sage pulls off the wrapper and gives me a piece. I pop it in my mouth. She takes a tiny bite from the bar, closes her eyes and swallows. I can't take my eyes off her chocolate lips. Thoughts race through my brain; my dick gets hard; Sage's lips on mine; Sages lips on my dick . . . I shake them away.

"Mmmmmm," Sage groans.

I stretch my tee shirt to hide my hard-on.

Bailey brings me back to school; his voice yanks me from Sage's chocolatefuck.

"Time to move on Joshua," he says. He raises his hand to pat my shoulder and changes his mind. Everyone knows not to touch me. "Next class?" Bailey says louder, his voice shakes.

Kids in the hallway hear and wait to see what happens. I don't like people who tell me what to do. Maybe I'll turn around, grab my lighter and burn the asshole's face? Watch flames lick his body? Maybe I'll stick pencils up his nose?

"Sure," I hiss. "Next class."

I take time. It pisses him. Bailey's shoulders are stiff – he's afraid. I laugh in his face and leave my signature.

"Thank you. Thank you. Thank you."

Bailey's face turns purple as I move down the middle of the hallway in the Red Sea.

They know what to do.

2

Bailey rushed into the school psychologist's office.

"Another one?" Dr. Wade said when he saw the art teacher. Wade was very young; it was embarrassing for Bailey to seek his support. The school psychologist finished his internship two years earlier and was immediately hired in upscale Memorial High School because his father was president of the school board. Wade looked more like Bailey's son than his colleague.

Bailey unrolled Joshua's artwork, his hands shaking. Bailey didn't know if he was angrier having to deal with the slim, tanned face of the psychologist or the grandiosity of the kid.

Joshua terrified Bailey. The kid's artwork, the ice in his eyes, and the rigid stance like a tiger stalking its prey, verged on inhuman. The alarms in his head went off – Joshua was dangerous. Wade, as well as the district, was more concerned about litigation from Joshua's parents, who had fancy degrees and attorneys. It was magical thinking. School and education was a political struggle; it was more important to secure the continuation of the institution than to identify the dangers within.

"It's his fourth one," Bailey said sharply.

Wade stared at the artwork. He didn't know where to take it. There were so many stories of school shooters and teenage violence; everyone was afraid. Joshua didn't talk much, threaten anyone, or write hit lists, and bomb recipes. Was it worth the risk of putting himself on the line when there were so few jobs open for school psychologists? He chalked up Bailey as another near-retirement teacher spooked by a kid who played too many violent video games.

"It was a dream," Bailey added. "This kid is in trouble. You know what the assignment was? To draw something that makes you happy. Happy? Last week it was Satan eating humans surrounded by skeleton cheerleaders. The week before . . ."

"I know," Wade cut him off. "This can be nothing or it can be pathological." He tried to sound professional. "I've talked to his parents many times. I spoke to them after Joshua was suspended for bringing a Laser Hawk sling shot to school. Dad said he took it away. Then I called the parents when Joshua wrote an English report praising Seung-Hui Cho, the student who killed thirty-two people at Virginia Tech. Calm down, nothing is going to happen. It's simply adolescent fantasy."

The two men stared at the drawing.

"Maybe it's a stage," Wade amended. "Acting out."

"Do you really think it's just a stage?"

Wade took a long time to respond. His job was more about mediating between administrators, teachers, and parents, than kids. SATs were coming up, college visits, student parking was a debacle, and he had to deal with *this*?

"Maybe not a stage," Wade conceded, "but don't quote me on that."

"What if he gets violent?"

"He's not getting violent. This is Memorial not the Bronx."

"Columbine wasn't inner city."

Wade ignored the comment. "The last time we called a committee meeting the mother threatened to sue."

"Don't they realize their kid is in trouble?"

"Maybe, maybe not. Either way, they don't want to believe anything is wrong. They don't want to be afraid."

"Don't kid yourself. The parents are *already* afraid. Probably for a long time."

"There's not much I can do without the cooperation of the parents. Joshua isn't hurting anyone."

"Yet."

"Maybe, but I have no choice. My job is to keep everyone informed. Working together and happy."

Bailey gingerly touched the drawing. "I'm going to leave this with you. Put it in his file – you'll have it when something goes wrong. This kid is a time bomb."

Tuesday

1

Cal stared out the front window of *Tree of Life*. It had been a long time since the fire. His thick wire glasses sank into his cheeks, making him look like an aging bibliophile – friendly, smart, and pitifully outdated. His brown hair had thinned, exaggerating his jowls and wrinkled forehead. He had gained over sixty pounds and wore loose-fitting clothes to hide his paunch; flapping fabric that made whooshing sounds when he shuffled through the store.

He felt every one of his fifty-two years – tired, disillusioned, and afraid of the future. He was compelled to stay rooted in the moment; stalled in the mediocrity of now. Cal shrugged and reached into his pants pocket for a fistful of *Petites Bouchées*, "little bites" of dark chocolate that Sage had introduced to him. Each bite was wrapped in red – the perfect size to pop in your mouth.

"Belgium chocolate," Sage told him. "Elegant and satisfying. Premium dark cocoa with an intensity that pleases the most passionate chocolate lover."

Cal had thanked her for the gift not knowing it would become another obsession in his arsenal. He kept boxes of *Petites Bouchées* everywhere – even on the work bench where he made his desktop bookshelves. He tore open the blood-red wrapper and popped the "little bite" into his mouth.

Thank you Sage.

"Chocolate is about life, Uncle Cal," she had explained. "Like the Tree."

Cal glanced at his watch. It was Tuesday, Joshua's day at the store. Ever since Kiran insisted that he share his business, the boy had helped out. Cal didn't pay him; Joshua didn't ask. Joshua's disinterest in money amazed Cal. When Cal was a boy, a few dollars earned meant everything. Joshua didn't care – he didn't care about most things.

There were no customers – *Tree of Life* was failing. Years ago, Cal believed that e-books would make his merchandise more valuable. He never thought that a wide array of online antiquarian and rare book sellers would surface in virtual storefronts armed with hefty discounts – faceless competitors nipping at his heels. Now it was a buyer's market. Secure with a title or author, buyers could find any book online at a lower price. Cal's command of history, knowledge of books, and love of literature was no longer a bargaining chip. Most people didn't have the time or interest to listen to his stories. The world of his parents, where history and imagination traveled hand-in-hand, was over. Most people were too busy to dream.

"Maybe you talk too much," Aldi suggested. "Most people are in a rush – they want to get in and out."

"There's always time for history," he argued. "It's who we are. History gives us depth and understanding, a window into ourselves."

Cal suspected Aldi was right, yet he couldn't shake the atavistic need to bring history alive; give each book a story of its own through the window into the author's soul. One of the few experiences that touched Joshua was when they shared books like *Lusitania* and *The Great Chicago Fire*.

Sadly, once Joshua became a teenager they no longer shared books.

Cal took a deep breath. Aldi's salary and the income from their investments kept the business afloat. For how long? Cal could see the not-so-far future when bills went unpaid and inventory gathered dust. He could even see *Tree of Life* boarded up.

Cal shivered. He and Aldi had discussed setting up an internet shop at home. Cal fought the idea; his soul was in bricks and mortar – beautiful book covers, sagging bookshelves, and ghosts. Although he no longer made money, Cal pledged to keep the business alive to his dying day. After that it would be Joshua's problem.

Joshua had calmed down. His grades were terrible but the school still passed him. There were no more dead cats, yet there were things about his son that Cal couldn't figure out. A look. A smile. Wearing biker clothes. Collecting magazines filled with photos of guns, knives and other weapons. A rare hug that felt aggressive rather than tender.

The school called to report erratic behavior – lying, suspected stealing, acting out. There was never any proof; only stories and ghoulish artwork, strange writing assignments, and Joshua's fascination for the macabre. Periodically, he and Aldi would show up in the school psychologist's office with Kiran as their advocate and argue that Joshua was learning disabled not emotionally disturbed. The school wanted an ED diagnosis – emotionally disturbed – to decrease their liability. Aldi was enraged, threatening to sue if they insisted. The school gave in and Joshua remained untreated except for an occasional visit with Kiran. Joshua was like *Gaboon Ebony*, the darkest colored wood in existence. It was so black that the grain was barely visible – nature's secret. The wood was used for things like knife handles and black piano keys in an odd juxtaposition of death and art.

Joshua came into view as Cal gazed absently through the store window. His son was with two kids who paused and stood in a tense huddle. Joshua talked while the two boys listened. The boys looked nervous; they stuck their hands into pockets and watched Joshua, never meeting his eyes.

Suddenly Joshua took a textbook and smashed it against his head.

What was the kid doing?

Cal knew he should run outside and stop Joshua. Instead, Cal waited to see his son's next move.

Joshua stopped dead for full effect and the boys edged back, glancing down the street as if they wanted to run. Body language was everything – it was clear that the boys were desperate to get away.

Joshua smirked.

He smashed the textbook on his head again.

Joshua lifted his right hand, curled three fingers into a fist, extended his index finger, and raised his thumb in the classic simulation of a gun. Grinning, he held his hand against one boy's head and clicked down his thumb as if shooting.

The boy turned deathly pale.

Joshua laughed.

The boys fled down the street. Joshua turned and saw Cal watching him through the window.

"Hi Daddy," Joshua grinned.

2

Daddy watches me from the store window. I show him. Talk up the assholes. Kids listen and don't dare ask questions. I brag about Bailey.

"Bailey's a fuck," I grin. "You know what I'm going to do?" I lower my voice and run it like a You Tube video. "I'm gonna blow his head off. I have this recipe for a bomb. Got it online. I mix like a fucking cake and when the asshole gets into his ugly car I'm going to . . ." I snap my fingers, "blow him into a thousand pieces. See? There's Bailey's foot," I point to the ground. "By the tree there's a finger . . ."

The kids turn gray.

"That's what I'm gonna do. Don't tell."

"No. We will never say a word."

"I like you now. If you ever rat on me . . ."

"Never."

I smash a textbook into my head. Their eyes bug. I smash it again. They breathe harder. It's fun to see their faces.

"You're not saying anything?"

"No . . . never, Joshua. Never!"

"If you say anything . . ."

I grin and make my hand like a gun. I press against one boy's head. "Click. You're dead."

The kid trembles.

"One day I kill myself and take some guys with me. You know what I mean? Like Columbine. I bet I kill a lot more people than they do."

"I bet you can," one kid hisses. "Gotta go. Mom's waiting for me."

"Me too." The other says.

They run. I watch. I dream about explosives, guns, knives, Laser Hawk slingshots. Maybe I buy guns on the street? Maybe I ask bikers at The Pizza Baas?

I see Daddy watching me through the store window.

Do you like the show, fat kike?

"Hi Daddy."

What would it be like to kill you?

A plan forms in my head like a dream. Kill the pig. Smash his skull. Slash his throat. Leave him bleeding at my feet.

Thank you. Thank you. Thank you.

3

Cal grinned. "I'm glad you're here, Joshua."

It was an odd thing. Cal *was* glad that Joshua had come to *Tree of Life*.

4

No customers. I look at books and pretend to dust. Daddy doesn't watch. I see titles. Some words are weird; David Kirschner says adopted kids lie because they feel lied *to;* steal because their identity is filched. I don't know what that means.

I wonder about my biological parents. Mommy and Daddy say they don't know. I ask but they lie. I hate when Mommy and Daddy lie. Maybe I'll tell them some bedtime stories about David Berkowitz, the Son of Sam and Kenneth Bianchi, the Hillside Strangler. Both are adopted. I dust more and meet Gerald Stano who kills forty-two women. One of the guys says that Spano was "the closest I've ever seen to a bad seed. It is like he was born without a soul."

I laugh.

Would you like to hear about him, Daddy?

My favorite is fifteen-year old Josh Jenkins who hammers his parents and grandparents. When his little sister wakes he takes her to a hardware store, lets her choose an Indian axe, and kills her with it. He watches TV, drinks root beer, and sets the house on fire. He's not on You Tube. I feel sorry for him. Josh Jenkins is only in stuffy books. I meet Robert Richardson III who shoots his father and dumps the body in a smelly pond. And Trey Sesler – Mr. Anime on You Tube – who studies and grades serial killers. When he's finished, Trey shoots his father, mother and older brother for fun. Lots of fun.

Daddy watches wondering why it takes so long to dust *these* books. Fat kike can't get it. Bundy, Dahmer, Rifkin – never boring like the stupid people I hear in school.

"What are you looking at?" Daddy asks.

He creeps up like a fucking freak. How does a fat slob move so quiet?

"Nothing."

Daddy sees my duster pause. It's on a book called *Sudden Fury* – Larry Swartz who murders his adoptive parents. Larry is the perfect son.

"I used to have that book in my office," Daddy says, "before it burned."

I move the duster and I'm Larry Swartz about to blast off my Daddy's head.

"You're a good kid," Daddy mumbles. "Sorry I'm not a better father." He pauses. "You hungry?"

I shrug.

He digs into his pocket. "Why don't you go over to The Pizza Baas and pick up something? Bring a slice back for me."

Daddy is sending me to The Pizza Baas?

"Anything you want."

He hands me a bunch of bills.

"Good boy." Daddy looks out the back door of the store at what's left of his office. He won't clean or rebuild.

Weird.

I grab the chance. Maybe one of the bikers at The Pizza Baas can tell how to kill? I run from the store like torpedo that sinks the *Lusitania*. The skinny assed kids are gone. When I reach The Pizza Baas it's like I come home.

Daddy shows me a book that tells the story of an unsolved murder at The Pizza Baas. Sal's throat is slit in the storeroom. No one knows who kills the owner. Some say Sal's ghost is there. Ghost hunters come in, eat pizza, and wait for Sal.

Nothing.

"Stupid legend," Mommy growls like a dog.

Maybe. Maybe not.

I go to the counter and order slices. The girl looks at me with mean eyes; she wears jeans, a dirty tee, and her hair in a black, greasy pony tail. She sticks her hand out for money. I put it in her palm, red with pizza sauce and oily crumbs. She wraps her fingers around the bills like a vampire.

There's a biker in the corner. He's not much older than me – nineteen? He rips off bites of pizza and stringy black hair falls in his face. I go over.

"What the fuck do you want?" He asks, not looking at me.

"A gun. I want to buy a gun."

"Get out of here, kid. You couldn't shoot a gun if you wanted."

"Could."

The biker stands up. Six inches taller. Muscles under his sleeveless tee, dirty beard, heavy jeans and Dr. Martens boots with steel toes and silver eyelets.

"If I tell you that you can't shoot a fucking gun, you *can't*."

Bitter rises from my gut and I want to off this guy right now.

The biker laughs. "Go back to your cartoons."

The biker leaves. I watch his back. I can't do anything. Yet.

My time will come.

Wednesday

1

I waited for Joshua in Walden Pond Park. I was near a circle of trees, not far from where the park fire burned years ago. I imagined that I was in the middle of a vast primeval forest alive with trees, plants, flowers, and noisy wildlife. Maybe that was what the park looked like a hundred years ago – a thousand years ago – a million years ago? The weight of time freed me. What did this moment mean when it sat next to so many others?

I think about what Joshua asked me, so many years ago.

You're not scared of me, Sage?

I skipped back to my reality. It was only a park. Years ago, after Joshua terrified everyone with Illusion, I had agreed to meet him on neutral ground in this secret place. It wasn't really secret – the trails were nearby, only a short distance from busy Merrick Road. We met as BFF and first cousins. Oddly, Joshua's bad times felt worse to me than him. We grew into teenagers and still 'hid' in the trees. I was always there for Joshua.

And Joshua?

Sometimes I wondered what it would be like to kiss Joshua. I knew it was wrong – he was my first cousin. I had already kissed and done lots of things with other boys, but Joshua was different. I never touched; only wondered.

Now it was too late.

Change had come between us. I was two years older and accepted into an out-of-state college. I had to attend to my own life. I clutched a small tote of chocolate, praying it would soften the news. Joshua wasn't like the other kids. Everyone whispered about

Joshua's threats to hurt and kill – himself, his parents, teachers, anyone in his path. They laughed nervously about his boasts to set bombs and emulate the Columbine massacre, but Joshua bragged about so many horrors that no one could possibly tell what was true, what were threats, and what were echoes from rap, video games, You Tube, and the nightly news.

During our quiet moments, I told Joshua that he wasn't bad. He listened. He wasn't the kid that Grandma Espie and Great Aunt Hanya warned me about. I saw something *good*.

I was his anchor and now I was abandoning him. Was there enough chocolate to salve the loss? I had decided to go away to college, live in a dorm, and leave Joshua behind. Was it the best decision? I would still be there whenever he needed me. In my heart, I knew that Joshua wouldn't get it – his world was concrete, controlled by what he wanted and didn't want. Life was a dance of his own needs.

So why did I love him?

I shrugged off the warnings from Grandma Espie and Great Aunt Hanya. I *knew* I was safe. What about the others? The people I loved, kids, teachers at school, and strangers walking down the street? What could Joshua do to them? The images in my head gave me chills. What would Joshua do without me?

Was I Joshua's keeper?

I had spent many hours with Grandma Espie, exotic chocolate on the table in front of us, arguing that point.

"Don't listen to me, "Grandma would say. "Listen to Great Aunt Hanya. She *knows*."

"She doesn't know everything."

"More than me. More than us."

"Not me."

"Open your eyes, *please*."

"I'm afraid of what will happen if I'm *not* here for him," I cried into a mouthful of single origin *Neuhaus Sao Tomé* made from the Forastero variety of cocoa beans. "He'll be so alone."

"It's a spicy flavor," Grandma observed. "One of a kind."

"Not better than *La Maison Du Chocolat*." I licked my lips at the thought. "A dark chocolate ganache macaron . . . "

Grandma agreed. We spoke the same language. "One of a kind," she said softly.

"Like Joshua, one of a kind. That's why no one likes him – why everyone is afraid."

"I wish I could see into the future."

"He'll never hurt me."

"I pray Joshua will never hurt you."

I shivered and grabbed another piece of chocolate as if it would protect me. I knew Joshua was broken yet I saw a spark buried inside.

"You have to be careful," Grandma warned yet again, nibbling a small square of *Chuao orange-a-go-go*. "People like Joshua can turn without warning."

"What do you mean?"

"You read about them in the newspapers every day. Like the pit bulls. BFF one minute, attackers the next."

I shook my head angrily.

"One day you wake up and it's over." Tears glistened in Grandma's eyes.

I thought about Grandma's words and knew that I had to tell him *now*, before his birthday party on Saturday. Joshua needed time to get used to the idea. My plan was to warn him when we were alone, like confessing a secret. Share the uncertain future as if it was a bond between us not a knife severing our connect.

I rehearsed the words but they sounded hollow.

I'm going to college, not leaving you. Nothing can tear us apart.

I knew what *had* to be said, but how? Joshua needed special words.

I peeked inside my small tote of chocolate, hoping to glean strength from the stash. Absently, I pulled out one of my strangest bars, *Vosges Red Fire*. One line stood out on the red-brown back cover of the bar.

Peace, love and chocolate.

I thought of the Mexican ancho, chipotle chilies, and Ceylon cinnamon that gave the chocolate distinction. Like Joshua, fiery and unpredictable, sharp and sweet all at once.

I popped a square of *Red Fire* into my mouth. Peace, love and chocolate. It seemed as improbable as red fire.

2

I go past kids playing soccer and kicking balls. I don't get it. The only fun is kick the ball *into* them. No one figures I'm smart. Fuckers think they get good grades and smarts. I laugh. What a mess up world. There are too many bikers with guns, too much violence, too much hate. No one should live in this world.

No one should live in this world but me.

I walk north into the park and follow the dirt trail in the trees. I like secret meetings with Sage. No one knows. No touches. Me and Sage. She's the only one in the world who gets me; who sees my greatness and shows no fear.

I laugh so loud that Sage hears me.

"Is that you Joshua?"

I break through the trees and stand in front of her.

"What's so funny?" she asks. "Why did you sneak up on me?"

"I didn't sneak up on you," I use my calm-Sage-down voice. "You didn't see me."

Sage shrugs.

I sit on the flat rock next to her – as close as I can take and stare at Dog's grave.

"I brought you chocolate."

"You always bring chocolate."

"This is special."

"You always say that."

Sage takes a deep breath. "You're going to like this." She hands me a square of chocolate. "It's called *Lindt – a touch of sea salt.*"

Sage waits for me to chocolate my mouth.

"The intensity of dark chocolate and the delicate seasoning of hand harvested *Fleur de Sel* sea salt crystals," she says.

I don't listen. The chocolate is popcorn at a movie. It keeps my mouth busy.

"You're not listening,"

"Fuck the chocolate," I snarl. "It's good. I like it. That should make you happy."

Sage is silent.

"Sorry," I say because Sage wants to hear. I know Sage's favorite words. Sorry – please forgive me – I'm really good inside. Sage likes that. It makes her happy. If only she ditches the fucking chocolate.

Sage makes kitten sounds to show her happy. "Thank you for apologizing," she says, patting my knee. I stare at her hand and she moves it quickly. Sage knows I hate to be touched.

Maybe if she grabs my dick it's OK?

"I have to tell you something."

"Yeah?"

She speaks so slow my skin crawls. "I'm two years older than you."

"Duh."

"I'm a senior which means I'm graduating this year."

"You want me to take you to the prom?"

"This isn't about the prom."

"What?"

"It's about college."

"You're going to live at home and go to school where Mommy works."

"No," Sage rubs her hands together and stares at Dog's grave. I follow her gaze.

"I don't get it."

"I changed my mind. I got a scholarship to an out-of-state school. A good one – it pays for a lot of things."

"I thought your parents rich – they don't need money."

"Two of us will be going to college. Me and Danielle. Two tuitions. Money is a lot tighter than it used to be – you know, like the store. They can't afford to pay for everything."

"I don't like talk about the store."

"Sorry. But I have to talk about college."

"So?"

Her voice rises. "Joshua – you have to hear me. I'm going away to school. I won't be here," she opens her arms to the park, "all the time."

Something inside starts to heat up like The Senator's lighter at my insides.

"I know I promised you but I can't turn this down. You understand? I know you understand."

The flame gets hotter.

Flames eat Dog. Flames eat Daddy's office. Flames eat chocolate. I speak but flames eat words. I open my mouth and fire comes out.

I leap off the flat rock.

"Understand," Sage cries, tears on her face. "I have to go away. It doesn't mean I'm leaving you – I'll always be there for you. It means that I won't be around *every* day. You can call or text or email or Face Book and I'll get back to you right away. I promise. I've never broken a promise before . . ."

Strange sound bubbles from me. Nazi Iron Eagles when kikes beg for mercy. The sound is high and fierce and inhuman.

"Don't," Sage pleads. "Don't cry. I'll be at your birthday party on Saturday. All of us will be there. Mom, Dad, Danielle, Grandma, Grandpa, and Great Aunt Hanya. Grandma Espie told me that she and Grandpa are sleeping over so they can have a birthday breakfast with you. Your first breakfast as a sixteen-year old. Isn't that great?"

"You promise me."

"I know I did," Sage lowers her head. "I know I promised you, Joshua, but things change sometimes."

"No."

"It's the same until the moment they change; the moment you see that the world will never be the same. It changes and then we move on in a new direction. Maybe better, maybe worse. Just different. We'll still be first cousins; we'll still understand each other better than anyone else. I'll always be there for you Joshua. I'll always love you. I promise."

Something deep inside surfaces. My world shifts into different. Voices attack. Please don't leave me. Please go back to the way it was. A different *she* doesn't hear. A different *she* doesn't feel. *She* shatters our connect. Her anger kills, rips her soul away. A voice breaks through. It's hard, ugly, stinging.

I hate you. I hate you. I hate you.

Die.

Everything moves in crazy, dizzy swirls.

Die.

My heart explodes into red. Something beats me over and over and over, changing waves that mix light, sound and *her* into sick, as if I'm inside her belly, waiting to be born into hell.

Sage whispers. "I'll always be there for you Joshua. Always."

The other *she* drowns Sage. I'm alone.

"I promise," Sage's voice is very far away.

A hiss rises from deep inside, snaking its way through my insides. The sound byte to my dreams. I run. From Sage. The rock. Dog's grave. I run from the park into streets and old houses and lawns and dead trees. I run and sweat and smell. My eyes blur. When I can't run, when I can't breathe, I sit on a curb like a fucking homeless in the middle of nowhere.

Maybe I've always been homeless?

3

I stared at my granddaughter's wild red hair, trying to comfort her. Sage cried, her face buried on my breast, her body trembling. I held her like an infant, knowing there was not much I could do. Like Mother and Robert Moses, some paths are inevitable.

"He ran away, Grandma," Sage wailed. "He ran away from me. I even offered him an entire *Vosges* bar of black salt caramel. He didn't care. *He didn't care at all.*"

"I'm sorry, so very sorry."

"I don't understand."

"None of us understands."

Suddenly the hamsa burned my neck – reminding me of the dreams. Night after night, faces, voices, and *him*. I see the darkness and the shadows between houses. I hadn't seen him for a lifetime but the words and images returned.

"I'm going to fuck you like you've never been fucked before. And when I finish, you know what you're going to say? Thank you. Thank you. Thank you." He laughed maniacally.

The memories are as vivid as if they happened yesterday, the words burning my mind.

"Before I give you the ride of your life, I'm taking this kike charm off your neck. It's in my way." He grabbed the hamsa, snapped the chain and tossed it on the ground. *"No one will protect you now."*

He yanked up my skirt and ripped off my panties. Then he unzipped his pants and pressed his raw, hard penis against my thigh. In a flash, thousands of years of rapes, massacres, pogroms, and the Holocaust flashed in my head.

It doesn't matter who you become, what you do, where you go. As long as any part of you is Jewish, no one forgets. They will find you.

"I'll show you what's good." Dutchboy panted, *forcing apart my clenched legs with his knee.*

I gasped. Eli had retrieved my hamsa. Dutchboy left me with his words.

I'll be back Espie, to settle our score.

I heard Mother's voice as if she were still alive.

The hamsa protected me all my life . . . and it protected you. Give it to someone you love very much. Someone who needs its protection.

I froze. There was someone else who said "thank you, thank you, thank you."

It was time. The hamsa told me. I had to protect Sage at all costs. I pulled her away from me and looked into those lovely young hazel eyes. "I have something for you, Sage."

Sage looked confused as I opened the chain that held the hamsa on my neck.

"It's protected me all my life."

"No – I can't take your hamsa."

I sighed. "My mother told me the story. The hamsa is ancient – some say it represents the hand of Miriam. Others say it's the sister of Moses. They all know it's the protective hand of God. It draws positive energy – life and happiness – and repels the evil eye and the angel of death."

"I don't . . ."

"The hamsa served me well. Mother gave it to me – and her mother gave it before that. Hundreds of years reaching back to Esperanza, our ancestor who was expelled from Spain."

"The one who killed the man murdering Jewish girls?"

"Yes."

"That's only a legend."

"No, Sage, it's truth."

"I don't understand."

"You will."

Sage trembled as I put the hamsa on her neck. Her skin was young, warm and smoooth.

"Esperanza," I smiled, tears filling my eyes. "The one with red hair and hazel eyes. The same as our red hair and hazel eyes. Esperanza's spirit is in this . . . Mother's spirit . . . and mine. We'll protect you from wherever we are. When it's your time, give it to someone you love very much. Someone who needs its protection."

"I can't . . ."

"You have no choice. It's my time to give it you; your time to wear it."

I closed the clasp.

Thursday

1

Cal stood at his worktable. He stared at his father's hammer, admiring the bright red handle, smooth, slightly rounded finished head, and long, curling claw. The material on his work bench was Bog Oak – a deep chocolate colored wood that laid for thousands of years immersed in a bog. The wood was expensive. Cal knew he spent too much money for his indulgence. It never mattered until now, when the business was failing. Cal didn't know what he was going to do without *Tree of Life*. Did his future lay behind a home computer screen, selling discount books online? He shivered.

Why? Why can't I see a tomorrow?

The front door to the house opened and then slammed shut. His heart pounded; beads of sweat broke out on his forehead. Everything trembled as if a wind, howling like feral cats, had blown into the Gothic. Although he didn't shout a greeting, Cal knew who it was.

Joshua was home.

2

Aldi stood at the kitchen counter chopping vegetables for dinner. A pile of diced red pepper was stacked alongside purple onions and yellow peppers. Next was the meat – a bloody, raw slab of boneless rib eye. The beef trembled beneath her fingers like something that had been alive not too long ago.

Tonight was wok night; Aldi would stir fry the meat and vegetables with Ponzu sauce. Everything would be served over microwaved brown rice. It was a good meal – Cal and Joshua loved it. She centered the slab of meat on the butcher block.

Now I have to worry about Sage.

Beth called Aldi two days ago to tell her that Sage was going to an out-of-town college. She won a scholarship and would be living away from home. It was good news, but Aldi's first concern was for Joshua. What will Joshua do without Sage?

Aldi raised her eight-inch *Forged Premio* chef's knife high over her head. She was angry at Beth. Why couldn't her sister keep the kid home? Beth had everything and Aldi – Joshua – needed help. Sage could be around until Joshua graduated high school and was better able to handle the separation; but it was always about Beth and her kids, never about Joshua. Angrily, she smashed the knife into the raw beef. Aldi wielded the knife again and again not realizing what she was doing.

Why can't Sage stay home?

The meat became a pile of jagged bits.

Why can't Joshua be like the other boys?

Aldi felt a sharp pain. The knife had slipped, nicking the tip of her index finger. She stared at her finger, fascinated with the knife, the meat, and her blood. She shook herself out of the stupor. The meat was ruined. She rushed to the sink and ran cold water over her finger; the water turned red as her blood trickled down the drain. She reached for a bandage in a small box next to the sink. It wasn't just Joshua this time – Cal was also in trouble. *Tree of Life* didn't have much time left. The bills were overwhelming and sales unable to sustain the business. Something had to be done. What would Cal do if he had to close the business – yet how long could they lose money without endangering everything else – their beautiful Gothic home, their lifestyle, and Joshua's many needs?

Aldi wished she could magically see into the future and know that everything would be all right. Cal would resolve his business problems, Sage would thrive at college, and Joshua would survive adolescence and turn into a handsome young adult.

Maybe he'll become a rock star manager?

No. Too much stress.

Maybe a businessman?

No. Aldi thought of Cal.

Maybe a doctor?

No. Too bloody.

Maybe Joshua will find his true self?

Aldi's stomach tightened. Impulsively, she scooped up the raw meat and tossed it in the garbage. No one was feasting on her blood – they were going vegetarian tonight.

The front door to the house opened and then slammed shut. Everything trembled as if a wind, howling like feral cats, had blown into the Gothic. Although she didn't shout a greeting, Aldi knew who it was.

Joshua was home.

3

We sit at the table.

Mommy, me, and the fat kike.

DR. JERI FINK AND DONNA PALTROWITZ

Mommy makes veggie crap and piles it on brown rice. The bitch forgets I hate brown rice. It crunches. I like white stuff but she doesn't give a fuck. I stare at my plate and wonder why there's no bloody beef or stringy chicken. Sage says that Mommy is a good cook.

I want pizza.

Daddy frowns. He's pissed. Why? He gets what he wants. He gets *Tree of Life*. He doesn't get teachers and school psychologists and social workers. He doesn't get tests or assholes that hate his drawings.

"Vegetarian tonight," Mommy says.

"I hate vegetarian," Daddy mumbles.

Mommy's face gets *dark* like a horror movie.

"It's all I have," she whines.

"All you have," Daddy yells. "You mean there's no money for food?"

"I didn't say that."

"You meant it."

"I didn't mean anything. All I said . . ."

"I know what you're trying to do," Daddy's voice rises. He doesn't yell much so this is a real treat. "You're saying we should close the business."

"I never said *that*."

"Not in so many words. You implied it."

Mommy looks at me for help. I laugh.

The fuckers are fighting.

"What are you laughing at?" Daddy snaps. He looks dark and red.

"Joshua's not laughing. He's minding his own business."

"Minding his own business? The kid never minds his own business."

"This isn't about Joshua. This is about the business and . . ."

I stand. "I'm outta here."

Mommy and Daddy look at me and I grin. I leave the table. Mommy and Daddy are stony silent. They don't get it. Sage leaves. Who cares about the business or veggies or their fight?

I escape to the den. I open the burnished black iron fireplace screen and throw in a few logs and a handful of fatwood – Daddy's favorite fire starter. I grab a long match, flame it, and toss. I sit and watch. The fatwood catches quick; flames curl over logs. My face gets hot. Daddy creeps up behind me.

"What are you doing?"

I stare at the fire.

"What the hell are you doing?" Daddy yells.

Mommy is behind him.

"He started a fire," she says.

"I told him never to start a fire. I don't *trust* fire."

"He's done it with you a dozen times."

"*With me.* Never alone."

"He knows how."

"I don't care. He shouldn't do it himself. He could do it wrong. The house could burn down like my office . . ."

The flames eat logs; hot and orange and yellow fill me.

"I told you," Daddy roars. "Never light a fire by yourself." Daddy puts his hand on my shoulder and tries to yank me to my feet.

I hate to be touched.

"Don't touch him," Mommy's voice is far away.

"I told you . . ."

Slow motion. I stand with his hand on my shoulder. I face the dribbling fat kike and his anger. I'm the flames curling around Daddy's anger. My arm pulls back, my hand is a fist, I swing into Daddy's face and feel his soft, fat cheek squish like a slab of raw boneless ribeye. His eyes go nuts and he staggers.

It feels good. I want to hit Daddy again.

And again.

Mommy screams. Like music.

I swing my fist into Daddy's gut, there's a whoosh of air, and he gasps and grabs his belly. One hand flies out to stop me. Grinning, I punch him again. I like the sound of Daddy gulps for air.

"Don't hit him," Mommy cries, putting herself between Daddy and my fist. I can't stop the swing and my fist lands on Mommy's arm.

Mommy isn't a fat fuck. It's not fun to hit her.

Mommy wails and Daddy rises like the dead and grabs my arm. He's stronger than I think. Maybe from lifting books? He twists my arm until it hurts. I try to get away from Daddy. I want to swing again but he's got my arm and any move I make will hurt. I balance and swing my leg, kicking him on the back of his knees. Daddy drops my arm and goes down like a sack of shit. I laugh and rub the kinks in my arm. I laugh and laugh and laugh. Daddy is on the floor, on his knees. I raise my foot and kick him in the ribs; there's a weird cracking sound. Daddy howls.

Mommy is gone. I hear voice from the kitchen.

Laughing. I kick and Daddy rolls on his side.

I return to the fire. It hugs me; orange fingers curl around my hands and arms and legs and chest. Wild flames fill me and power me. Daddy rolls but there's no stopping me.

The door opens and I hear Mommy's voice.

Help me. Help us.

Two cops rush in. One is a big guy with a belly that strains buttons on his uniform. He grabs my arms, twists them behind my back and drags me from the fire. Something cold around my wrists. Handcuffs. The fucking cop handcuffs me.

The second cop looks at Daddy. Her straight brown hair is pulled back into a tight ponytail. Loose hair falls on her face.

"Are you okay?" she asks.

Daddy can't talk.

"Fat fucking kike," I say calmly. "He touches me."

The big guy with the belly yanks my arms. It hurts. "Keep your mouth shut," he growls. Mommy stands in front of the fire – a black shadow in yellow and orange.

The bitch cop helps Daddy to his feet. It would be fun if my arms didn't hurt so much. The cop with the belly holds me.

"You OK?" The bitch cop asks Daddy. "Do you want me to call an ambulance?"

Daddy shakes his head. "No."

"I'm Officer Paula Tinto," she says. "Your wife called for help. She was right. You need it." She looks at me. "Tell me what happened."

Daddy opens his mouth and I scream.

Fuckyou cocksucker motherfucker assholekike.

The cop with the belly yanks my arms. It hurts bad.

"He's Officer James McBride," Tinto continues. "Is that your son?"

Daddy nods. "Joshua."

"Would you like us to take him in; charge him with assault?"

Mommy makes a sound that reminds me of Dog. "No. No. No."

Tinto glares at Mommy. Daddy doesn't know what to say. Five people in front of my fire and Daddy looks at me.

"Are you OK Joshua?"

I answer sweetly – I don't want the cop yanking my arms again. "Yeah."

"Are you going to hit me again?"

"No."

"No. No. No." Mommy wails.

"He won't hit again." Daddy gasps. "The kid just lost his temper."

Tinto shrugs. "I think we should take him in. You can discuss this tomorrow when everyone cools down."

Daddy's face swells from my punch. "Are you OK Joshua?"

No one speaks.

"Don't arrest him," Daddy says finally. "Take off the cuffs. I'm not pressing charges. This was a family dispute and we can figure it out on our own."

Tinto shakes her head. McBride frowns.

"Yes officers," Mommy echoes, "a family dispute. We're all fine. Thank you for coming but we'll be OK now."

McBride hesitates; he looks at Tinto.

"Thank you for helping us," Daddy adds. "We're fine."

"Wait," Mommy finds her voice. "Before you release him . . . Joshua, you have to promise you'll go to Kiran to deal with this."

Kiran? Fuck, I don't need to see that bitch.

The four grown-ups are silent, all eyes on me.

I nod.

"No," McBride snarls. "I want to hear you say it. I want to hear you agree to what your parents ask."

I take a deep breath. "Yeah."

"Yeah what?"

"Yeah I'll go to Kiran."

McBride snaps my arms really hard. "If you hit your father like that again," he whispers in my ear, "it will hurt a lot more – like this." He jerks my arms and it feels like he's breaking them. I cry out in pain.

"I'll call Kiran now," Mommy says softly. She gets the phone and leaves a message. "We have an emergency – you must see Joshua tomorrow. If not, he's going to jail."

"Juvie hall," McBride mutters. "Where the bastard belongs for beating up his father."

"Done," Mommy clicks off the phone.

"Done," Daddy agrees.

You're done.

Stick a fork.

Friday

1

Kiran scanned her office as she waited for Joshua. The telephone message was chilling.

We have an emergency – you must see Joshua tomorrow. If not, he's going to jail.

Kiran sighed. She still had a copy of the note pinned to his blanket when he was abandoned in the Safe Haven program. She had been so sure that a good Jewish family would make him prince of the house, and Joshua would be fine. Since then, Kiran had learned a lot about Reactive Attachment Disorder. It could be treated, but it could also grow and turn into much darker problems. RAD might be totally resistant to intervention, particularly if the brain was already organized to withstand the humanizing impact of conscience and empathy. Was it possible to diagnose that kind of deficit in early childhood? Perhaps concrete tests like MRI brain pattern analyses would one day identify mental illness. Until then, it was left to subjective evaluation and conjecture. Who would sentence a toddler to a serious, lifelong diagnosis on that kind of evidence?

I couldn't do it. Then or now.

Kiran recalled an article she read, several years after placing Joshua with Aldi and Cal. The authors, Levy and Orlans, maintained that children with severe attachment disorders are "violent psychopaths in training."

Kiran shivered. What had she done?

Experience taught Kiran about *healthy* children. Psychoanalyst and Pediatrician, Donald Winnicott believed that parents don't have to be perfect – just good enough – to raise a child. What if the *child* came with deficits that weren't identified? Deficits that fed into the parent's issues like guilt or loss from infertility?

As the daughter of a celebrity, she and Morgan worked very hard to remove themselves from the media that hungered for sound bites, revealing photos, or embarrassing slips. It took more work than anything else in their lives. Maybe it was beyond science – metaphysical – fate or karma? She was born under the shadow of The Senator . . . while Joshua was born under the ghost of his mother. Kiran had always felt a strange, inexplicable connect . . .

Kiran sighed. Her office, unlike her experience, remained the same. It was still a large space with a beautiful view. The spacious waiting room now had an updated leather couch and chairs. The bookshelf was no longer beneath the camera. Her oak desk, once painfully neat, was buried in paper files that she was reluctant to store on the computer. The play area was filled with new toys, most with lights, sounds, and voices. Life moved on.

Except Joshua.

2

The waiting room door opened. She watched the cam as Aldi and Joshua entered. They sat on opposite ends of the couch. Kiran took a deep breath. This was going to be a long session. She stood up, opened her office door, and smiled.

"Come in."

Kiran looked at Aldi – her eyes were red and her face sagged. She looked old, worn, and defeated. Joshua stared at the floor. Mother and son came into her office and sat as far from each other as possible.

"It's nice to see you guys."

Aldi cut her off. There was no room for chat. "Cal didn't come because he's hurt."

"Hurt?"

"Maybe a broken rib – lots of bruises – he looks like a punching bag."

Joshua stared out the window.

"Joshua did it. Don't let him tell you anything else. Joshua beat up his father – I had to call the police to make him stop." She paused. In a very small voice, she whispered, "and he hit me too." Aldi rolled up her sleeve and displayed a large mottled bruise on her arm.

Kiran stared at Joshua's work.

"Sorry Mommy," Joshua said. "I didn't want to hurt you. Only Daddy."

Joshua's eyes were blank.

"Is that true? You beat up your dad and hit your mom?"

Joshua stretched out his legs. "Sorry Mommy but not sorry Daddy."

"What happened?"

Aldi told the story, from the moment she began chopping vegetables to Joshua leaving dinner, and starting the fire. "It wasn't just the fire. Cal was in an awful mood – the business is going under. When he saw that Joshua started the fire without his permission, he lost it."

"I beat the shit out of him," Joshua added. "I'm here because I didn't want to go jail. The cop kept hurting me."

There was a long silence.

"The cop had no right to hurt me."

Aldi stared at her hands, tears streaming down her face. Kiran watched Joshua. He stood up and wandered around the room. He picked up a toy truck and smashed it against the wall; it splintered into a dozen pieces.

"Remember when I do that?"

Aldi's shoulders buckled.

"Why don't you sit in the waiting room," Kiran said softly. "Close your eyes and rest a bit. Joshua and I need to talk."

Aldi met Kiran's eyes. It was the look of a deer caught in a car's headlights. "Help him," Aldi said softly. "Please – he needs so much help." She turned to Joshua. "I love you. Whatever you do, always know that."

Joshua didn't respond.

Aldi left the room and Kiran turned to Joshua.

"No," he laughed, "I don't have a razor blade in my mouth."

3

This stuff sucks. Daddy deserves it. Why blame me? Drag me to Kiran's shithole? The fat kike asks for it.

"Joshua." She speaks soft like always. "Sit down, we have to talk."

I sit.

"What happened yesterday?"

"I beat the shit out of Daddy."

"Why?"

"You know the story."

"I want to hear it from you."

"He pisses me off. I have rights. No one yells me. I start a fire – I do it all the time."

Kiran holds her breath. "When?"

She really doesn't want the answer.

"Lots of times. You don't want to know. You're married to a fucking fireman."

"We're not talking about my husband."

Joshua shrugged.

"Why?"

"He won't let me start fires."

"Isn't that a safety thing?"

I look window.

"Is there anything else?"

"Sage. She blows."

"Why?"

"She goes to college. Leaves me."

"Is she really leaving you?"

"Yeah."

"Did she say that?"

"Yeah. She's the only one."

I stop.

"She's the only one who?"

Strange words leak. "Sage is like *her*. Leaves me like I'm a sack of shit. Hates me."

"Who is *her*?"

"I ask Mommy and Daddy about *her*. They lie. They say they don't know anything. She leaves me with cops. Done. That's all they know. I don't believe them. They lie."

"Are you talking about your Birth Mother?"

Not sure. Words stick in my mouth.

"Your parents aren't lying. No one knows about your Birth Mother."

"Bullshit. I know. She's pretty like Sage. She never leaves – someone steals me and gives me away. She never leaves."

Kiran looks away. "I don't know if this will help." She goes to desk. Opens folder. The world is in slow motion – a television replay with fuzzy voices. She pulls out a paper.

"This is a copy of the note pinned to your baby blanket – when you were one day old and left at the police station."

She hands me an old scrap of red checkered cloth with a crumpled napkin pinned to it. I read words.

Please give my baby a safe haven. His name is Joshua.

I stare. I read. It takes a long time before I get it. Pictures and voices thunder. Disconnect.

My world shudders, pounded from the outside.

Die.

It hurts. Everything moves in crazy dizzy.

Die.

I won't die. I won't let her kill me. Hard and dark and evil.

I'll live. At all costs.

No one can stop me.

Kiran waits.

Kiran waits forever.

I crumple the only connect with my Birth Mother and bury it inside my pocket next to The Senator's Lighter.

Kiran makes a big mistake. Sage makes a big mistake. Mommy and Daddy makes a big mistake. I shape shift – fire, no blood. No organs, no heart, no soul. I'm the disconnect.

Thank you. Thank you. Thank you.

Saturday

1

It's supposed to be special. My sixteenth birthday. It feels ugly and dirty and angry and full of hate. They come for cake and gifts and smiles and birthday hugs.

I hate them. I want to be alone, a Nazi Iron Eagle. Dance with skeletons and hanging men and spiders and bugs and Satan. That's what I want but they don't give it to me. Mommy and Daddy and Grandma and Grandpa and Great Aunt Hanya and Auntie Beth and Uncle Thomas and Danielle and . . . Sage . . . come to smile and laugh and stuff fat faces for *me*. I don't know *me*. Only a momma who threw me away.

I see her face – the bitch who throws me away. I see her face in dollars, fancy houses, cars, and fucking men. Any man. Like my father who *makes* me. A shadow, evil grin, ugly in his eyes. That's what I celebrate. My sixteenth birthday.

The day they threw me away.

2

Aldi put the finishing touches on Joshua's birthday cake.

Happy 16th Birthday Joshua.

It was a homemade red velvet cake filled with custard and covered with dark chocolate butter cream frosting. Aldi's hands trembled. It had been an awful week. Cal was still limping, popping pain pills, and sporting red bruises on his face. Tears flowed and Aldi didn't know where they came from or when they would stop

– endless tears and relentless grief. She wiped her face; a few tears spotted the chocolate butter cream. Aldi stared with horror at Joshua's cake. Where were they headed? What was Joshua's future?

Aldi shook her head and smoothed out the tear stains on the frosting. She couldn't get rid of the pictures in her head – Cal on the floor, the fire blazing, Joshua smiling, cops, and handcuffs. It was too much. She tried to block the sound of Cal's screams, Joshua's grunts, the splat of Joshua's fist sinking in his father's gut, and the crack of Cal's rib.

"I think we need to send Joshua . . . somewhere," Cal had said. Aldi and Joshua had just returned from Kiran. Joshua was supposed to be upstairs while Aldi prepared dinner. "We can't do this anymore."

"Do what?"

"This," Cal spread his arms to encompass their world. "Joshua. He's too much for us."

"The learning disabilities . . ."

"Learning disabilities? Enough, Aldi. There's a lot more *wrong* with Joshua than learning disabilities."

Not on his sixteenth birthday.

"He'll be fine – he needs time . . ."

"Open your eyes for once. He's had time. Joshua needs more help than we can give him. There are places for boys like him – places where he can live, go to school, and get help from professionals."

"You're not sending my son away."

"We don't have a choice."

Aldi caught a slight movement from the corner of her eye –
Joshua was listening to them.

"No," Aldi screamed but she didn't believe her words. Cal would
break her down. Cal stormed off to his workshop and Joshua crept
catlike up the stairs.

Now, staring at the botched birthday cake, Aldi wondered how
long she could stand in Cal's way. How long could she keep Joshua
home? The future felt like a black hole.

A tiny voice crept into her consciousness.

What would life have been like if I kept The Senator's baby?

Aldi turned away from the cake and sobbed like a little girl.

3

Cal hid from Aldi. He stayed in his workshop and closed her
out. He leaned against his work bench and stared at his tools.
He was too physically hurt to build anything. Every part of him
screamed – Joshua had torn him apart in both body and spirit.
Gently, reverently, Cal took the claw hammer from its peg on the
wall. He felt the connect with his father.

How could he send Joshua away? How could he *not* send Joshua
away? After all the reports, the problems, Kiran's words . . . how
could Cal lose him like he lost his parents and brother? How could
he lose him and *Tree of Life*?

He gripped the hammer as if it would ground him. There were
more important things to consider. Cal had to reason through his
next step – they could send Joshua to the best residential school

for psychological and educational support; professionals who would know how to handle the kid. He and Aldi had spent endless amounts of time, money and effort, yet no one could tell them how to heal the beautiful, broken child who was their son.

4

I sorted through my chocolate. What should I bring to Joshua's birthday party? It was a bittersweet celebration. I knew I had hurt Joshua deeply. I heard his voice.

I don't get it, Sage. I don't get it.

Where was Joshua going without me? I held up a *Urzi Cioccolato* bar – a sharp Italian mix of extra fine dark chocolate and a *Coffee Huehuetenango* bar – Guatemalan, with intense floral aromas and a hint of walnut.

Joshua, like the chocolate, was strange and dark. I had fought to bring out something good buried deep inside my first cousin. I *knew* it was there. Didn't everyone have a streak of goodness – a positive energy that soothed the soul? I touched the hamsa on my neck. I had never been scared of Joshua until I told him about my college plans. The scream – a primal animal cry that rose in his gut shook my soul. I had never heard anything like it. It made me remember Grandma's words when she gave me the hamsa.

"We'll protect you. From wherever we are."

Why do I need protection?

I sighed. It was so sad – Joshua was both powerful and vulnerable; I had touched something deep within and he reacted in a gut-wrenching scenario. There were no answers.

It's going to be okay.

It has *to be okay.*

5

They come for dinner. Mommy's beef and sliced mushrooms with chopped tomatoes, artichoke hearts, thick gravy and a splash of *Pinot Noir*. Mommy chops for a long time with her *Forged Premio* to kill vegetables and meat. There's red wine they let me sip because I'm sixteen years old, crusty Italian bread with garlic and oil, and string beans with the ends cut off. Everyone laughs – Mommy and Daddy and Auntie Beth and Uncle Thomas and Grandma Espie and Grandpa Eli and Great Aunt Hanya and Danielle and Sage.

Daddy starts a fire in the fireplace.

Sage wears Grandma's hamsa.

"Why?" I ask.

There's weird silence. "Grandma gave it to her," Grandpa says softly.

"Why?" I ask again. No one answers.

"It looks good on her," Grandma says lamely.

I can't look at Sage. Everyone knows it. Everyone knows *why*. They're not angry at her – they're angry at me. I should understand. *They* don't understand. They're stupid and fat and can't see the greatness in me. Who cares about a fucking hamsa or going to college? I listen, I don't talk, they make me angry. The heat rises – orange and yellow tongues.

Dinner is over and Mommy brings birthday cake. Chocolate. I hate chocolate.

"Sixteen candles," Mommy says, "and one to grow on."

"Grow on?"

"Good luck," Auntie Beth grins. "A good luck candle."

There's silence.

"Let's light the candles," Mommy sighs. She strikes a match and lights candles. Sixteen flames and one to grow on. "Make a wish and blow them out."

"I don't want to blow out the fire."

They surround a fucking chocolate cake and wait for *me* to stop the fire?

"Joshua," Sage whines, "it's your birthday."

"I'll help you," Daddy says. Red bruises flicker in the candles. He blows out my fire.

Fucking fat kike. Why did you do that?

They sing Happy Birthday to You, Happy Birthday to You, Happy Birthday Dear Joshua, Happy Birthday to You.

Mommy cuts cake and everyone eats but me. I won't eat Mommy's cake and I won't eat chocolate again. No one says anything – they pretend it's a good time. They're afraid of the birthday boy. Great Aunt Hanya watches me, head tilted. What does the old bitch think of me now?

By eleven they're gone. Mommy cleans kitchen and goes to bed, Daddy turns off lights, Grandma and Grandpa climb stairs to guest bedroom. I stay alone in front of the dying fire. The flames flicker and crack and dance.

"Are you coming to bed?" Daddy asks.

"Not now," I say. "Soon."

Daddy nods. He wants to talk but he stops. Words never said. He climbs the stairs to bed.

I'm alone.

I reach into my pocket. The crumpled ball of paper and red checkered cloth that Kiran gives me is next to The Senator's lighter. I pull out the paper, flatten it, read, then toss it into the fire.

The paper and red checkered cloth turn black, catches fire, flares like a fireball, then dies. Goodbye Joshua's Momma.

I wait until everyone settles upstairs. When there's no more noise, I go to kitchen. I find Mommy's *Forged Premio*. I pick up and put it in front of the fire. I go to Daddy's workshop. I take his claw hammer, stroke the red handle, and put it next to the knife. I sit and watch.

Hammer. Knife. Fire.

Sunday morning

1

I sleep.

I dream of devils, ghosts, dead men, Nazi Iron Eagles, and You Tube.

My eyes pop. It's Sunday, three in the morning. Outside the sky is dark; inside the last embers of fire burn.

I stand and slide Mommy's *Forged Premio* in my deep pocket. I hold Daddy's claw hammer in my hand. I face stairs.

Daddy moves upstairs. He's in the hall. I climb the stairs; they creak and moan like men waiting for execution. Daddy is in bathroom. Words dance.

Daddy's last pee. Daddy's last flush.

Illusion in the toilet bowl. Dog in the park. Daddy's office.

Daddy opens door and sees me. He's not surprised or scared. I see sleep in his eyes and bruises on his face.

"Joshua – you're still up?" Daddy asks.

Daddy's last words.

I raise the claw hammer that belongs to Daddy's father. I bring it over my head. It moves slow motion. Daddy freezes. His eyes go from the hammer to my face and back again. He tries to speak but only spit dribbles from his lips. An instant that lasts forever.

I smile. The last seconds of Daddy's life; a lifetime in my head. Pictures. Sounds. Stories. Daddy realizes what's happening and he reaches out fat fingers to grab the red handle.

He's too slow.

I sink the hammer in his skull. There's a strange, cracking sound like a nail splitting a bookcase. Daddy wants to speak. There are no words left. I hit him a second time and he doesn't see it. His knees buckle and he falls. Graceful. Not like Thursday when he drops hard like a sack of shit. Not like Thursday when Daddy howls.

His chest moves. Up down. Up down.

Daddy breathes. The fucker doesn't give up.

I twirl the hammer around and smash with the claw side. His head, his eyes, his chest. Blood spurts everywhere – a fountain of red. Shit smell fills the hallway. Daddy poops in his pants.

There's a new sound. Blood gurgling.

My tee shirt is red with blood. I have to wash it – get out the blood and smell of Daddy's shit. Easy to erase Daddy. I look up and Mommy watches.

"Joshua," she wails, "what have you done?"

Mommy's last words.

Her face twists with sad and hurt and silly tears. Choking sounds and hand grabs. I don't want to kill Mommy but I have to. She watches as I swing the bloody claw hammer. Her eyes go from Daddy to me to hammer. She doesn't want me to stop – Mommy can't take what's happening. It gives me time. Poor Mommy. I really don't want to kill her. She's sad about Daddy so I'll be good to Mommy and end her sad.

I swing the claw hammer into her head. She drops to the floor, no words, no screams, no spit. Mommy makes a thud when she falls on Daddy. She doesn't need the claw side of the hammer.

Bye Mommy.

I stare at them – dead Mommy and Daddy. Mommy's unhappy about the mess. She hates dirty things. It's good and right and they have it coming. I raise the claw hammer because it's mine now.

Grandma Espie shows. She wears silly nightgown and grabs my face in her two bony hands. "Joshua stop. You don't want to do this."

No one touches me.

I swing the hammer. Grandma is easier than Mommy and Daddy. Her old bones crack. My heart pounds – I'm powerful – I make life and death. There's a cool sound when the hammer hits her skull and she falls in silence; her hazel eyes see nothing.

Now Grandpa. I go to the guest bedroom. He takes out his hearing aid and leaves it on the night table so he doesn't know anything. Still asleep, I do him in bed before he wakes up. I go back to the bodies in the hall. Mommy stirs, groans.

Not dead.

I pull out the *Forged Premio* and slash her throat. Her blood bubbles like a pot of boiling water. I do Daddy and Grandma Espie.

The Gothic is silent.

I stab the bodies over and over because it's fun. The knife sinks like boneless rib eye on Mommy's butcher block. In. Out. I stab until my arms are tired. When I finish, I go back to Grandpa. The bed turns red from his blood. A beautiful thing like my drawing at school.

2

I drag bodies into Mommy and Daddy's bedroom. They're heavy and my arms hurt. Mommy and Daddy on bed, Grandma and Grandpa on floor. I turn on the light so I can see my work. Beautiful. Blood covers everyone and everything. I drop the claw hammer on Daddy's belly, stick the *Forged Premio* in Mommy's breast.

My tee shirt and jeans are bloody, my hands and arms are bloody, brain is all over me – bits of slimy, nasty-smelling stuff. I go to the bathroom where Daddy takes his last pee. I strip off my clothes and dump into the hamper. I save The Senator's lighter. I shower and watch the blood go down the drain.

Now I am clean.

I dry myself in a fluffy white towel – Mommy's favorite. I take The Senator's lighter and walk naked down the hallway and into my bedroom for clean clothes that Mommy folds for me. I dress in jeans and another tee shirt. I pocket The Senator's lighter. Mommy is happy I wear clean clothes. Daddy is happy I have The Senator's lighter.

I go downstairs and into the kitchen and drink a bottle of cold root beer. I think of Josh Jenkins and fill a plate with chocolate chip cookies. Mommy tells me not to eat all the cookies, they might make a belly ache.

I grin. Mommy can't stop me – I can eat all the cookies I want.

I take everything into the den.

You'll stain the couch Mommy says.

I push away the fire screen. There are only a few logs but I put them all in the fireplace with lots of fatwood. You can't build a fire by yourself, Daddy says.

Watch me.

I build a big, hot, roaring fire. I watch TV, drink root beer and eat all of Mommy's homemade chocolate chip cookies.

Thank you. Thank you. Thank you.

Sunday Night

Joshua Jenkins.
Tyler Hadley.
Alex and Derek King.
Robert Richardson III
Trey Sesler.

And me.

1

It's time.

"No one is home" I call to empty house. "No one will ever be home."

I look at bodies in the bedroom and save the picture in my head. It's sad I have to fire them. I look for money and find few hundred dollars. I pack money and extra tee shirts in my backpack. It's large and black with no design. I think about taking claw hammer and *Forged Premio* but they belong to Mommy and Daddy.

I go into the turret playroom, sit at the laptop, and post my last You Tube. I pour lighter fluid in trails and designs that make Bailey proud. I throw fatwood. I soak couch and beds and write *kike* on the walls with black markers.

Everything is ready. I take The Senator's Lighter from my pocket. Daddy is happy. I flick it and stare at the flame. It's a beautiful flame that shoots out of brass, the engraved White House with The Senator's signature. I touch flame to the fatwood, logs, and lighter fluid.

The fire snakes through the house. I watch. The Gothic burns. I'm in the middle and I don't want to leave. The flames draw me close and the heat burns my face. Something kicks in like Daddy's office. It knocks me back into smart.

Get out.

I sneak out the back door as the firemen arrive. There are people on the street watching. Cops try to control the spectators – stuff them behind a barrier. I look for Tinto and McBride but don't see them.

I slip into the crowd to watch.

2

The stars were gone.

Morgan leaped from the truck. The night sky was gray with smoke. Vehicles choked the street, red and blue lights blinked crazily. Cries, sirens, and the hiss of fire permeated everything. There were too many people, trucks, and noise. Mesmerized neighbors were herded behind police barriers.

The fire was winning.

Morgan's heart pounded. He hated the late shift when he left Kiran and the kids at home and went to work. There was no choice. That was the job.

Morgan had to mobilize, get ready for a battle that both terrified and thrilled him. Fire was evil – control made it powerful; out-of-control made it deadly.

Morgan took a deep breath. He had a really bad feeling about this one. People's voices echoed in the distance.

"It's yours Morgan," the Chief waved him on.

Morgan signaled to his partner. "We're going in, Hector."

The two men put on respirators; there was no hesitation or fear. Morgan felt the eyes of people standing behind the barrier, riveted on his back. He saw his buddies balancing heavy hoses as they streamed water on the house.

It had once been a beautiful home. Between the smoke and flames, Morgan could see the graceful lines of an old Gothic with a turret, wrap-around porch, and bold windows. Someone would mourn this house. Someone lived here and perhaps died here.

He raced up a single concrete step with Hector following close behind. Morgan took a deep breath and went through the front door. Thick smoke choked the house, rising from his hips to the ceiling. He dropped to his knees and crawled through the sprawling rooms searching for people. Curtains were bathed in flames, couches collapsing to ash, wood furniture eaten by fire. Someone had taken great care to make this a beautiful home. Someone had loved it. Morgan hoped they were out – that the flames hadn't devoured them along with their home.

Morgan headed for the stairs, once elegant wood risers with a classic, heavy oak handrail. He tested the first step. It was solid. Waving to Hector, Morgan slowly negotiated each step. At the top there was more smoke than fire. Breathing deep into the respirator, Morgan began the upstairs search.

There were a lot of doors. He entered the turret room first. It was empty except for a seared bulletin board and a charred laptop. Morgan signaled to Hector and headed to the next door. It was an empty bedroom. He searched two more bedrooms before hitting the master. The door was closed and Morgan pushed it open cautiously in case fire was locked inside. There was only smoke and he couldn't see very far.

He made his way toward the bed where a few flames struggled to survive. They hissed and spit at him but couldn't win. He saw the first body.

"We have a victim," Morgan said.

Morgan hit something with his foot as he moved to the other side of the bed. He looked down. It was another body. He touched it and felt rigor mortis – the person had been dead before the fire started.

"This is a crime scene."

On the bed were two more bodies, one with a knife in it.

"Four victims," Morgan took a deep breath. "Murdered."

3

Morgan emerged from the house. He took off his respirator and wiped the sweat from his face. He looked at the crowd. There was a kid . . .

He hesitated. Morgan didn't want to make a mistake.

After a few moments, the fireman yelled and pointed to the kid with caramel-colored hair and blue eyes. "That's *him*," Morgan roared. "That's the kid who started the fire."

No one moved.

Morgan wasn't going to let the kid get away this time. He lunged at Joshua. There was no time for the kid to escape. Morgan tackled him to the ground, calling for backup. Joshua struggled, punching and kicking.

Joshua pushed himself up and tried to run. Morgan was too fast. He grabbed the kid and pinned him in the dirt. Something popped out of his pocket. Cops and firemen rushed to help. They pulled Morgan off the kid and yanked Joshua to his feet.

"He's the fire starter," Morgan said breathlessly. "And this isn't the first time."

Everyone froze. Morgan was accusing a *kid*. How could that be?

"There are four dead bodies in that house," Morgan added, glaring at Joshua.

Joshua smiled.

After the police left with Joshua; after the fire was out; after the Gothic was reduced to charred remains; Morgan remembered that something had popped out of the kid's pocket. He returned to the spot where he tackled him. Morgan kicked through the dirt, leaves and ashes.

Suddenly he saw something shiny. He bent down for a closer look. It was an old cigarette lighter. Proof? Morgan picked it up. The old-fashioned brass lighter had a drawing of the White House on the front. He flipped it over.

His father-in-law's signature was engraved on the back.

Beyond Evil

1

He was pleased. The Jews were fucked.

The Senator relaxed in his spacious Park Avenue office and listened to the news. He sat in his favorite luxury recliner – a custom-made power seat in dark mahogany leather. No one entered the office but him, the cleaning lady, and his staff. His wife, daughter, son, and visitors were prohibited without invitation. Requests were filed with his secretary – a stern, homely woman who never smiled. She resided in a large waiting room, filled with his framed campaign posters, community service awards, political commendations, plush seats, and a muscled, uniformed security guard during work hours.

In a locked drawer he kept photos taken by a heartless private investigator. They were all there – Espie and her entire family, Ayla and Mack, and most prominently, Joshua.

Joshua.

The headlines screamed at The Senator.

Teenager Murders Family

The Senator smiled. "Thank you, thank you, thank you," he said to the empty office.

The Senator was proud of his grandson. The demon boy had honored his family tree. Blood libel was satisfied; extermination given new life.

The Senator believed in the domino theory, calculating that one human action will predictably lead to another, given the right context. Remove one piece and everything comes to a dead halt. Keep the flow and events follow like a chain of dominos, each one pushed down and in turn, pushing down its neighbor.

He controlled the game. If there was a problem, The Senator would step in and make it right. He had the power and money to do anything he wanted; target anyone he chose.

Like Joshua.

The Senator picked up a single domino from the ivory set on the side table next to his recliner.

He rubbed the domino between his fingers and thought about his legacy.

The story began long before he was born, when 15th century Jewish sisters killed his people. The Senator appreciated the ancient vendetta that had been passed down through his bloodline. It was right for himself and his kin. Whether today or 500 years ago, The Senator was destined to play the game. Fortunately, one didn't need to murder with knives and guns anymore. The kill required his intelligence, cunning, and dominoes. The Senator's objective was simple – fuck the Jews and win the game.

Only once did he lose the game; only once when the dominoes flew out of his control. The Senator would never forget or forgive the skirmish between their homes in Levittown when they were adolescents. Espie was his – to do as he pleased. He trapped her against the wall, and spoke like an Inquisition soldier.

"Before I give you the ride of your life, I'm taking this kike charm off your neck. It's in my way." He grabbed the hamsa, snapped the chain and tossed it on the ground. *"No one will protect you now."*

He yanked up her skirt and ripped off her panties. Then he unzipped his pants and pressed his raw, hard penis against her thigh. Thousands of years of triumphs – rapes, massacres, pogroms, and the Holocaust validated his power. It was his turn – he was the hero, intent on murder and revenge.

Espie went limp, no longer able to resist.

"I'll show you what's good." He panted, forcing his knee between her clenched legs, drunk with his fire over past and present.

Then he heard a sound like a raging mastiff. Huge hands grabbed his shoulders and pulled him off – hands that were detached in the shadows. The hands flung him on the ground. He screamed like a feral cat. Feet kicked him, generating howls of pain.

It was Eli – the man Espie would marry and use to spawn another generation of Christ-killers.

"I'll be back, Espie," he promised, so many years ago. "To settle our score."

Now they were all dead.

He unzipped his pants and clasped his penis. He rubbed, harder and faster, until he cried out in an orgasm of blood and murder.

2

I paused next to the car, plunging into a lifetime of memories.

I need my own ending.

I touched the hamsa on my neck. Grandma Espie's voice whispered in my head.

Esperanza and Chana's spirits are in this, Sage. Along with Mother's and mine. We'll protect you from wherever we are.

She had warned me to be careful; Joshua could be dangerous. Why didn't I listen? Could I have changed anything? Grandma Espie had protected me at the cost of her life.

I sighed; tears filled my eyes and I rubbed them away angrily. Why Joshua? Wasn't the chocolate enough? I recalled what I said to Grandma.

Joshua would never hurt me.

The words haunted me.

I slipped into my car, turned on the ignition, and headed to Smithville. I needed to see, one last time, the Gothic that had spawned such evil. It was only a few minutes' drive – a trip I had taken countless times. I parked in front of the remains, starring at the black, charred skeleton of Joshua's house.

"You think chocolate fixes everything," Joshua said.

"I know that."

"How do you know?"

"I just know."

"Asshole."

"You don't scare me, Joshua."

"I had fun cutting your doll. You should do it."

My eyes filled with tears. "No one can be that bad."

"Try me."

I took a deep breath. Would Joshua always haunt me?

Oddly, the fireplace had survived the fire – a reminder of what had once been. Blackened bricks littered the foundation. People came by the house and scooped up souvenirs. Many sold pieces on the internet.

Authentic Relics From Mass Murderer House

For a while, the remains had to be protected, but that died quickly like the stories in the news and on You Tube. Eventually the house was forgotten and people moved on.

Slowly, I climbed the concrete front step where we had once sat. The flames had never touched it, as if Joshua had magically preserved it as a memorial to *before*.

I shivered.

Why Joshua? Why?

Would I ever stop asking that question? I saw Joshua on the step and then on the flat rock in the park. I heard his voice.

Thank you. Thank you. Thank you.

All I could ever do was offer chocolate.

I wandered past the step into what had once been the heart of the house, trying to place the rooms – the kitchen, the den, Uncle Cal's workshop.

Could I have stopped it?

I fell to my knees, crying, recalling our talk in the park. I heard Joshua's primal, inhuman cry. It was too much; too much to live with – and I was determined to move on.

"You have to go on," Great Aunt Hanya demanded. "Joshua ended four precious lives. Don't let him end yours."

Mom agreed.

"We'll face it together," Hanya promised.

I knew that whatever they said – whatever anyone said – I would never forget.

Taking a deep breath, I felt the hamsa grow warm on my neck. Did Grandma know what was going to happen?

It will protect you.

All of those spirits, reaching way back into Spain, including the murderers, were with me.

They're all here.

I turned my back on the dead Gothic. I went to the car and drove slowly past the dusty, boarded remains of *Tree of Life*. Twenty minutes later I arrived at the courthouse. Ignoring the reporters and news trucks, I entered the building where Joshua's fate would be sealed.

3

In the courtroom, Joshua sat at a very crowded defense table. His legs were sprawled, his face uncaring. He didn't react when the prosecutor called him a "sixteen-year old killing machine." Social media buzzed with opinions. One tweeter wrote that "it's a waste of taxpayer's money to keep him alive." Another bemoaned that "juveniles can't get the death penalty."

The words didn't touch Joshua. He stared into nothing.

No conscience. No empathy. No remorse. No compassion.

He played with his fingers and the papers on the table. He met no one's eyes, had no expression on his face, and denied hating the people he killed.

He smiled when witnesses described the murder scene. Shrugged when Kiran's husband, Morgan, explained the fire and how he saw Joshua. The Police Detectives played a video with his confession. It had leaked and gone viral on You Tube.

"The world's really messed up," Joshua said.

"Why?" The detective asked.

"There are too many problems – too many gangs – too much hate." Joshua sighed. "I don't want my family to live in it anymore." He grinned. "I did them a favor."

4

The Judge sat above everyone in the courtroom. He squared his shoulders, smoothed his black robe, and pounded the gavel. He glanced at The Senator sitting in the front row, flanked by body guards. Kiran and her husband sat behind him. The Senator nodded and the judge began.

"This has been a rampage of mass murder that was vicious, savage, and almost incomprehensible. Words can't adequately describe our loss and sympathy as a community. For the protection of society, as well as the surviving members of the victim's family, Joshua will spend twenty-six years to life for each murder, plus eight years for arson – a total of one hundred and twelve years in prison. No parole. The sentences will run consecutively so Joshua will never be able to kill again. The living victims will not have to be afraid." He looked at me, compassion in his eyes.

I sat between Mom and Great Aunt Hanya.

"It's over," Great Aunt Hanya whispered. "You don't have to be afraid."

Would it ever really be over?

I got up to leave the courtroom. Hanya offered to come with me, but I told her I wanted to be alone. She understood. We became closer after the murders. I pushed my way through crowds, press, and spectators. I located my car and left, headed for the cemetery.

I had to visit Aldi, Cal, Grandma, and Grandpa one last time. I put a *La Maison Du Chocolat* ganache called *Mont-Blanch* on each grave. It was soft and sweet with a note of Kirsch. Some people say it had a dizzying effect.

"Rest in peace," I said softly.

I armed myself with a *Quito Macaron* and headed back to college.

5

I watch Sage leave the courtroom. She won't look at me. Why? I didn't bloody her.

For a moment we're sitting on the front step. Talking. Sage's words echo in my head.

"No one can be that bad, Joshua."

The fire rises in my body; in my father's books; in the place I once called home.

No one can be that bad, Joshua

Sage.

She was wrong.

Go back in time!

Books 4-7 explore how evil thrived in the past. Meet the modern descendants in the first three Broken Books and follow their haunted family trees back through time.

Enter the 17th century when Dutch New Amsterdam is run by tight-fisted Peter Stuyvesant. Twenty-three Jews arrive from Brazil, fleeing the Portuguese Inquisition. They face an agonizing struggle for their rights. Suddenly a psychopath surfaces, threatening everyone in the young settlement. The Dutch blame the atrocities on a gentle Munsee Indian while mutilated animals and children stain Jew's Alley. Who is the psychopath? Why is he or she attacking Jews? *Book 4*

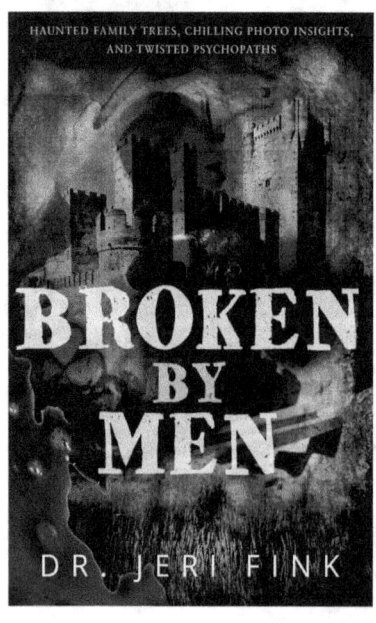

Hannah and Esperanza flee The Inquisition, joining the expelled Spanish Jews in 1492. They find refuge on a tiny Portuguese farm with two old Christian peasants. A traveler discovers the sisters and turns them into the royal soldiers. Simao, a psychopathic soldier and his band arrive on the farm and evil spreads. How can the young girls survive the men? *Book 5*

Esperanza is kidnapped by the King's soldiers. She joins a group of 2000 Jewish children shipped to the malaria-infested African Island of São Tomé. The Portuguese soldiers in the camp are brutal, using children as sex slaves. Esperanza and her friends are grabbed by the newly arrived psychopathic soldier, Simao. Can they escape fever and the evil of kings? *Book 6*

The Broken Saga begins in 1492. The Tapiadors are Conversos (Secret Jews) who are betrayed to The Inquisition. Armed soldiers arrive to arrest them. The parents push their two daughters through a hidden trapdoor into a tunnel that leads to safety. The soldiers drag the parents to the torture chambers. Can the parents save their children and survive the torture? *Book 7*

Books can be purchased in ebooks or print at amazon.com or hauntedfamilytrees.com/books

Check out Books 1-3 to explore how evil thrives today in haunted family trees.

The first book in the series finds media psychologist, Dr. H (Hanya) and her great-niece and intern, Sage, in Manhattan. Dr. H is a national TV psychologist with her own talk show, seen around the world. A psychopath emerges from the audience, with a gun and a vendetta. *Book 1*

It's 1992 and a spine-chilling birth is destined for evil. Who is Joshua and where does he come from? Is Sage really in love with her first cousin? What does The Senator have to do with the story? Does Grandma Espie know what's coming? *Book 2*

Everyone is terrified of Joshua. Drowned cats, dissected squirrels, and burning dogs are his playthings. No one knows what the child thinks or will do next. The Senator, Aldi and Cal, Sage, and Grandma Espie, among others, return in this blood-curdling thriller. *Book 3*

Books can be purchased in ebooks or print at amazon.com or hauntedfamilytrees.com/books

Meet The Book People

Dr. Jeri Fink

Author, Photographer

I was eight years old.

Faces were penny candy – endless shapes and flavors. Colors throbbed in rhythmic neon lights. My world was a rush of stories written in black-and-white composition books.

There were so many ways to *see* things. The Oak outside my window was big and powerful – or shaky, like a typical New York City tree. I could take a sliver of black charcoal and make the same tree magically come alive on paper. My characters moved through plots more animated than the people next door. I aimed my camera and shot images that no one else noticed.

They called me a free spirit.

I wanted to share, but most of my friends were in different spaces. We went to college and they talked about business, teaching, and making money. I wanted to know about art, lucid dreaming, and the human spirit. We grew up, got jobs, and evolved into families. There were spouses and children; Little League and PTA. I had my family, a home in the suburbs, and a family room painted purple. When everyone dined on backyard barbeque, I preferred Chinese noodles. I stashed chocolate fudge brownie ice cream to weather blizzards, and talked about books no one read at the neighborhood dinner parties.

I never quite *fit*.

I went back to school and became a Family Therapist to help people negotiate their lives. I worked with everyone from "normal" to psychopath. My friends thought *I* was crazy.

Oddly, I was always ahead of my time. I played on the internet before most people had ever heard the word. I developed, along with a group of far-reaching thinkers, the idea of psychotechnology – the psychology of technology. My nonfiction book, *Cyberseduction*, was written long before eHarmony and match.com went viral. Donna Paltrowitz and I worked with kids on books where children became a voice in their own literature. We called the series *The Gizmo Books*. Gizmo and his "sister" Coco were Labradoodles – an Australian breed which most people at the time, including the vet, never knew existed.

Instead of simply growing up, my eight year old *evolved*. In the twenty-five books I've written since then – nonfiction, children's, and adult fiction – I'm still an author with faces, colors, and stories fueling my imagination.

The *Broken Book* series is a culmination of who I am – the voices of those who entered my mind and heart; the people who pass me on different paths, with their own haunted family trees; and the photos that tell their stories.

Welcome to my world.

Visit us at www.hauntedfamilytrees.com
Email me at jeri@hauntedfamilytrees.com

Purchase books in ebook or print at www.amazon.com
or hauntedfamilytrees.com/books

Donna Paltrowitz

Author

I won!

It was a school writing contest for the best autobiography, and mine came in first. I was in the sixth grade and had no clue about writing. The words flowed effortlessly from my head to the pen. The teacher described my essay as an intricate process rich with ideas, humor, and the desire to connect with others.

Years later, I graduated from college, worked as a teacher in Brooklyn, N.Y. and realized that teaching children to express themselves wasn't the seamless process that I had envisioned. This was a different generation with needs that required new techniques and resources. Spending my days in the classroom with children, and nights earning a Master's Degree in reading, I discovered the latest, most effective techniques to make the entire room smile.

I became a reading specialist. My ideas flowed into developing tools to motivate struggling readers. Focusing on real experiences that kids encountered in their schools, streets, and homes, I created a humorous reading series for children with limited reading vocabularies. Along with my husband Stuart, also a New York City teacher, we wrote the *I Hate To Read Series* – 24 books with music, rhymes, and smiles – long before rap and Miss Piggy became a hit.

We connected with children throughout the country and the English-speaking world. Subsequently, we wrote the *Work World Series* for teenagers trying to make sense of their lives. When schools finally wired up, we designed *Computer Crossroads* and *Mystery Mazes* – software series that engaged young people in reading, laughing, and making fun choices.

Watching my own three children grow up, I realized that reading connections continually evolve. While teachers and administrators tried to lead children to relevant topics, kids were more interested in what their peers were saying. Children connected when they were given a voice. Dr. Jeri Fink, my friend, neighbor, and a LI family therapist agreed that children should have the chance to bring their own literature to life. Together we brought children's issues, words, and artwork alive in *The Gizmo Books*. We visited classrooms with Gizmo, a 100 pound therapy dog and his "sister," Coco. The Labradoodles came from Australia, driving their messages to connect children, parents, grandparents, and schools half way around the world.

Meanings of words shift with the passage of time while the human need to connect remains unchanged. What was once called interacting with friends, neighbors, and colleagues, is now social networking – sharing our messages, bonding with others in the world, and helping us all to feel warm and fuzzy on the inside. Both the teacher and child inside me continue to seek new pathways into the present, as well as the past. That is the heart of *The Broken Book Series*-stories rich with ideas, photos, and the desire to connect with others. Whether child or adult, our families bind us to the good, the bad, and the ugly of our histories. Wander through these adult novels for an insightful connection to the haunted family trees that make us who we are.

Visit at www.hauntedfamilytrees.com
Email at donna@hauntedfamilytrees.com

Purchase books in ebook or print at www.amazon.com
or hauntedfamilytrees.com/books

Derek Murphy
Book and Cover Designer

Derek Murphy started a book editing company while working on his PhD in Literature, but soon began using his background in fine arts to help clients with their book covers. Derek believes in using art to create an immediate emotional connection with readers, and get them invested in your story before they even open the book. Check out Derek's website at:

www.creativindiecovers.com

book web publishing, ltd.

Book Web Publishing, ltd. was founded in 2000 to provide a forum for creative and unique works in children's and adult literature.

Purchase books in ebook or print at <u>www.amazon.com</u> or hauntedfamilytrees.com/books

Thanks!

How do you thank everyone who was part of a project that spanned six years, six books, and tens of thousands of photographs? It's a daunting job. If we leave anyone out please forgive us – there was an overwhelming number of people who have been part of our lives and work during the creation of the *Broken Books* series.

First, our families:
Our husbands, Richard Fink and Stuart Paltrowitz.

Our children and their children:
Russell, Laura, Mason, and Emma Fink
Adam & Blair Paltrowitz.
Darren Paltrowitz and Melissa Andreev
Shari Paltrowitz

Stacey, Greg, Johnny, and Nicky Rossi.
Meryl & Tony Waters.

Our extended families:
Harvey Fink
Robin March
Bruce and Jillian Milman
Ronnie & Sherry Milman
Sandra Roth
Barbara & Chris Woolley

Many thanks to our friends and supporters who listened to our stories, drowned our troubles in chocolate, and were always there when we needed them. Sheryl Ackerman, Jay Braiman, Dr. Barton Cohen, Sheldon Crooks, Cindy DiBiasi, Joyce & Joel Feldman, Melissa Friedman, Dr. Edward Fryman, Pat & Mary Ann Hannon, Howie Hutchinson, Janet & Rich Kam, Dale Kranz, Bill Kumar, Jerry & Jill Lash, Dr. Carol Levy, Joan Mirabella, Gail Orlick, Barbara Saks, Rachel Teplin, John Viollis, and Sandra Weiss.

Special appreciation goes to our readers: Fern Friedman, Laura & Russell Fink, Craig Oldfather, Dr. Sandra Roth – our experts: Nancy Allegretti, Phoebe Balsky, Mary Ann Hannon, Margaret Mendel – our proofreader: Pat Hannon – and our designer, Derek Murphy.

Thanks to Sue and Ken Yaeger, who generously shared their experiences and insights to bring these books alive.

Much gratitude to Tim Jaccard, AMT Children of Hope Foundation/Baby Safe Haven Program who explained his program and how important it is for all of us.
A tasty thanks to *Chocolate Works of Bellmore-Merrick, La Maison Du Chocolat,* and *Nom Wah Tea Parlor.*

Our gratitude goes to the many artists, authors, filmmakers, investigative reporters, photographers, psychologists, researchers, social workers, theorists, and videographers who informed our work, empowering us to accomplish our mission.

In loving memory of Judy Becker, Dora Eisenstein, Edna Fink, Joseph March, Gladys & Larry Milman, Ruth Roth, Dr. Sandra Roth, and Vincent Meo.

Last, but not least, thanks to our readers who joined us in this amazing journey.

Publisher's Note

www.ingramcontent.com/pod-product-compliance
Lightning Source LLC
Chambersburg PA
CBHW061545170626
46811CB00001B/93